's Library Collector's Library Collector's Library Collector's Libra
Library Collector   brary
's Library Colle   Libra
Library Collector   brary
's Library Colle   Libra
Library Collector's Library Collector's Library Collector's Library
's Library Collector's Library Collector's Library Collector's Libra
Library Collector's Library Collector's Library Collector's Library
's Library Collector's Library Collector's Library Collector's Libra
Library Collector's Library Collector's Library Collector's Library
's Library Collector's Library Collector's Library Collector's Libra
Library Collector's Library Collector's Library Collector's Library
's Library Collector's Library Collector's Library Collector's Libra
Library Collector's Library Collector's Library Collector's Library
's Library Collector's Library Collector's Library Collector's Libra
Library Collector's Library Collector's Library Collector's Library
's Library Collector's Library Collector's Library Collector's Libra
Library Collector's Library Collector's Library Collector's Library
's Library Collector's Library Collector's Library Collector's Libra
Library Collector's Library Collector's Library Collector's Library
's Library Collector's Library Collector's Library Collector's Libra
Library Collector's Library Collector's Library Collector's Library
's Library Collector's Library Collector's Library Collector's Libra
Library Collector's Library Collector's Library Collector's Library

Collector's Library

THE SHERLOCK HOLMES
EVERLASTING DIARY

'Sherlock Holmes, the most famous
man who never lived.'

ORSON WELLES

The Sherlock Holmes Everlasting Diary

Compiled by
ROSEMARY GRAY

Illustrations by
SIDNEY PAGET

Collector's Library

The Sherlock Holmes stories were published
between 1887 and 1927

This edition published 2015 by Collector's Library
an imprint of Pan Macmillan
20 New Wharf Road, London N1 9RR
Associated companies throughout the world
www.panmacmillan.com

ISBN 978-1-9096-2133-6

Compiled by Rosemary Gray

I

A CIP catalogue record for this book is available from the British Library.

Typeset by Antony Gray
Printed and bound in China by Imago

Visit www.panmacmillan.com to read more about all our books
and to buy them. You will also find features, author interviews
and news of any author events, and you can sign up for e-newsletters
so that you're always first to hear about our new releases.

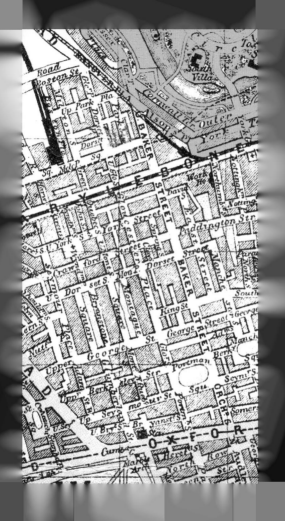

JANUARY

January 1st

Arthur Ignatius Conan Doyle was born in Edinburgh in 1859 into an Irish Roman Catholic family of Norman descent. He was the second of ten children. His father, a talented painter, was a trained architect, employed in the Board of Works. 'My father's life was full of the tragedy of unfulfilled powers and underdeveloped gifts.' His mother was a French scholar who took a fierce pride in her Foley lineage; her hobby was heraldry. The family was distinguished on both sides. His grandfather (famous as 'HB') reinvented the art of political caricature, and his uncles John and Richard both became well-known artists and illustrators. It was Richard Doyle who drew the cover design for *Punch* which was used for a hundred and seven years.

_____

_____

_____

_____

_____

_____

_____

January 2nd

January 3rd

Charles Altamont Doyle, Arthur's father, was a life-long depressive whose alcoholism seriously destablised the children's early years, many of which were spent in a modest tenement flat. 'When my grandfather's grand London friends passed through Edinburgh they used, to our occasional embarrassment, to call at the little flat "to see how Charles is getting on". In my earliest childhood such a one came, tall, white-haired and affable. I was so young that it seems like a faint dream, and yet it pleases me to think that I have sat on Thackeray's knee.' In 1868, thanks to help from his wealthy uncles, he was sent to the Jesuit preparatory school for Stonyhurst College. He went on to five years at Stonyhurst and a final year at a Jesuit school in Feidkirchin in Austria. He emerged an agnostic in 1876.

_____

_____

_____

_____

_____

_____

January 4th

View of Edinburgh in 1822

_____

_____

_____

_____

_____

_____

January 5th

Doyle studied medicine at the University of Edinburgh Medical School, where one of his professors was the distinguished forensic surgeon Dr Joseph Bell. Deeply impressed by Bell's remarkable ability to deduce a great deal about a patient from very few facts, Doyle was also struck by his angular appearance and immense energy. In addition to being a brilliant doctor, Bell was also an amateur poet, a sportsman and a birdwatcher. In later years, he took some pride in having been the inspiration for Sherlock Holmes.

_____

_____

_____

_____

_____

_____

_____

_____

_____

January 6th

'How in the world can you say that?'

'If you examine it carefully you will see that the pen . . . has spluttered twice in a single word and has run dry three times in a short address, showing that there was very little ink in the bottle. Now, a private pen or ink-bottle is seldom allowed to be in such a state . . . But you know the hotel ink and the hotel pen, where it is rare to get anything else. Yes, I have very little hesitation in saying that could we examine the waste-paper baskets of the hotels around Charing Cross until we found the remains of the mutilated *Times* leader we could lay our hands straight upon the person who sent this singular message.'

The Hound of the Baskervilles

_____

_____

_____

_____

_____

_____

January 7th

On 20 September 1879, Doyle published his first academic article, 'Gelsemium as a Poison', in the *British Medical Journal*, but in his spare time he was trying his hand at short stories, one of which, 'The Mystery of Sasassa Valley', a story set in South Africa, was printed in *Chambers's Edinburgh Journal* that same September. As an author, he chose to write under the name Conan Doyle, using one of his middle names to make a compound of his surname, which strictly speaking was simply Doyle.

_____

_____

_____

_____

_____

_____

_____

_____

_____

January 8th

Holmes was seated at his side-table clad in his dressing-gown, and working hard over a chemical investigation. A large curved retort was boiling furiously in the bluish flame of a Bunsen burner, and the distilled drops were condensing into a two-litre measure. My friend hardly glanced up as I entered, and I, seeing that his investigation must be of importance, seated myself in an armchair and waited.

'The Naval Treaty'

January 9th

Once qualified, and eager for adventure, Doyle signed on as ship's doctor for a voyage on the Greenland whaler *Hope of Peterhead* in 1880. A year later he sailed as ship's surgeon on the SS *Mayumba* on a voyage to the West African coast. Subsequently he drew on these experiences of life at sea for stories such as 'J. Habakuk Jephson's Statement', a fiction based on the famous mystery of the *Mary Celeste*.

_____

_____

_____

_____

_____

_____

_____

_____

_____

_____

January 10th

A splintered boat and a number of crates and fragments of spars rising and falling on the waves showed us where the vessel had foundered; but there was no sign of life, and we had turned away in despair when we heard a cry for help, and saw at some distance a piece of wreckage with a man lying stretched across it. When we pulled him aboard the boat he proved to be a young seaman of the name of Hudson, who was so burned and exhausted that he could give us no account of what had happened until the following morning.

'The *Gloria Scott*'

January 11th

Ready to embark on his medical career, in 1882 Doyle set up in practice in Plymouth with his friend George Budd, but the partnership was short-lived and Doyle moved to Portsmouth alone and put up his plate at 1 Bush Villas, Elm Grove, Southsea. Business was slow and while waiting for patients he had ample time for his writing. In 1890, in pursuit of greater success in his profession, he went to Vienna to study ophthalmology. On his return to England he took a consulting-room in London's Wimpole Street, 'but not a single patient crossed the threshold'.

_____

_____

_____

_____

_____

_____

_____

_____

_____

January 12th

An instant later I heard him running down, and he burst into my consulting-room like a man who is mad with panic.

'Who has been in my room?' he cried.

'No one,' said I.

'It's a lie!' he yelled. 'Come up and look!'

'The Resident Patient'

_____

_____

_____

_____

_____

_____

January 13th

It was while he was in Southsea that he met and married his first wife, Mary Louise Hawkins, 'Touie', the sister of one of his patients whose tragic case he had handled with great compassion. His writing was already meeting with a degree of success and his wife was enthusiastic and encouraging. By 1885 his work had been published in *London Society*, *All the Year Round*, *Temple Bar* and the *Boy's Own Paper* and had been taken up by the prestigious *Cornhill Magazine* and attracted the attention of the critics: '*Cornhill* begins the New Year with an exceedingly powerful story . . .'; '*Cornhill* opens its new number with a story which would make Thackeray turn in his grave . . .'

January 14th

Morris drank, and his white face took a tinge of colour. 'I can tell it to you all in one sentence,' said he. 'There's a detective on our trail.'

McMurdo stared at him in astonishment. 'Why, man, you're crazy,' he said. 'Isn't the place full of police and detectives and what harm did they ever do us?'

'No, no, it's no man of the district. As you say, we know them, and it is little that they can do. But you've heard of Pinkerton's?'   *The Valley of Fear*

January 15th

His medical practice may not have prospered but his writing career was beginning to take off. However, he felt that what he must write if he were to achieve real literary success was a novel. For a central character, he had conceived the idea of emulating writers he admired, such as Emile Gaboriau and Wilkie Collins, and inventing a detective. 'It was about a year after my marriage that I realised I could go on doing short stories for ever and never make any headway . . . but could I bring an addition of my own?'

_____

_____

_____

_____

_____

_____

_____

_____

_____

January 16th

It was a fine, thick piece of wood, bulbous-headed, of the sort which is known as a 'Penang lawyer'. Just under the head was a broad silver band nearly an inch across . . . It was just such a stick as the old-fashioned family practitioner used to carry – dignified, solid and reassuring.

The Hound of the Baskervilles

_____

_____

_____

_____

_____

_____

_____

_____

_____

_____

January 17th

'I thought of my old teacher Joe Bell, of his eagle face, of his curious ways, of his eerie trick of spotting details. If he were a detective he would surely reduce this fascinating but unorganised business to something nearer to an exact science. I would try if I could get this effect . . . What should I call the fellow? I still possess the leaf of a notebook with various alternative names. One rebelled against the elementary art which gives some inkling of character in the name and creates Mr Sharps or Mr Ferrets. First it was Sherringford Holmes; then it was Sherlock Holmes. He could not tell his own exploits so must have a commonplace comrade as a foil – an educated man of action who could both join in the exploits and narrate them. A drab, quiet name for this unostentatious man. Watson would do. And so I had my puppets and wrote my *Study in Scarlet*.'

Memoirs and Adventures

January 18th

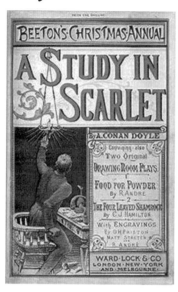

January 19th

Conan Doyle submitted the manuscript of *A Study in Scarlet* to several publishers. At Ward, Lock & Co., the chief editor, G. T. Bettany, gave it to his wife (a writer herself) to read. Her verdict was unequivocal: 'This man is a born novelist! It will be a great success!' Her husband's letter to the author was cautious : 'We have read your story and are pleased with it. We could not publish it this year as the market is flooded at present with cheap fiction, but if you do not object to its being held over till next year we will give you £25 for the copyright.' When the author pressed for more generous terms, the response was disappointing: 'In reply to your letter of yesterday's date, we regret to inform you that we shall be unable to allow you to retain a percentage on the sale of your work as it might give rise to some confusion. The tale may have to be inserted, together with some others, in one of our annuals. Therefore, we must adhere to our offer of £25 for the complete copyright.'

January 20th

We had reached Baker Street and had stopped at the door. He was searching his pockets for the key when someone passing said: 'Good-night, Mr Sherlock Holmes.'

There were several people on the pavement at the time, but the greeting appeared to come from a slim youth in an ulster who had hurried by.

'I've heard that voice before,' said Holmes, staring down the dimly lit street. 'Now, I wonder who the deuce that could have been.'

'The Scandal in Bohemia'

January 21st

In spite of the small sum offered and the long delay, Conan Doyle accepted Ward, Lock's terms. ('I never at any time received another penny for it.') *A Study in Scarlet* appeared in *Beeton's Xmas Annual* for 1887 and received good reviews in the *Scotsman* and the *Glasgow Herald*. Conan Doyle wrote to Joseph Bell: 'It is most certainly to you that I owe Sherlock Holmes . . . Round the centre of deduction and inference and observation which I have heard you inculcate I have tried to build a man.'

January 22nd

Our visitor sprang from his chair. 'What!' he cried, 'you know my name?'

'If you wish to preserve your incognito,' said Holmes, smiling, 'I would suggest that you cease to write your name upon the lining of your hat, or else that you turn the crown towards the person whom you are addressing.'

'The Yellow Face'

January 23rd

Robert Louis Stevenson wrote enthusiastically to Conan Doyle from Samoa: 'My congratulations on your very ingenious and very interesting adventures of Sherlock Holmes . . . can this be my old friend Joe Bell?' Parallels were drawn between Holmes and Edgar Allan Poe's 'masterful detective' C. Auguste Lupin, who had been a hero of Doyle's since his boyhood. Today we see Holmes as the forerunner of a host of fictional sleuths from Lord Peter Wimsey and Hercule Poirot to Inspector Morse.

_____

_____

_____

_____

_____

_____

_____

_____

_____

January 24th

'The attack was made by two men armed with sticks, and Mr Holmes was beaten about the head and body, receiving injuries which the doctors describe as most serious. He was carried to Charing Cross Hospital, and afterwards insisted upon being taken to his rooms in Baker Street.'

'The Illustrious Client'

January 25th

In the late summer of 1889, Philadelphia publisher Joseph M. Stoddart, managing editor of *Lippincott's Magazine*, invited Conan Doyle and Oscar Wilde to dinner at the Langham Hotel in London. 'The result of the evening,' remembered Doyle, 'was that Wilde and I promised to write books for *Lippincott's*. Wilde's was *The Picture of Dorian Gray*, a book which is surely on a high moral plane, while I wrote *The Sign of The Four*, in which Holmes made his second appearance.' Doyle and Wilde got on famously, and Doyle reported that it had been 'a golden evening'.

January 26th

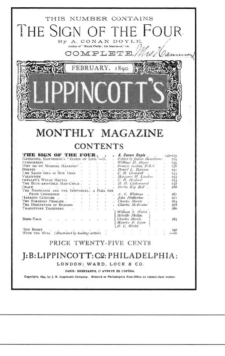

January 27th

'A number of monthly magazines were coming out at that time, notable among which was *The Strand*, then as now under the editorship of Greenhough Smith. Considering these various journals with their disconnected stories it had struck me that a single character running through a series, if it only engaged the attention of the reader, would bind that reader to that particular magazine. On the other hand, it had long seemed to me that the ordinary serial might be an impediment rather than a help to a magazine, since, sooner or later, one missed one number and afterwards it had lost all interest. Clearly the ideal compromise was a character which carried through and yet instalments which were each complete in themselves, so that the purchaser was always sure that he could relish the whole contents of the magazine. I believe that I was the first to realise this and *The Strand Magazine* the first to put it into practice.'

Memories and Adventures

January 28th

'Ames, I understand that you have often seen this very unusual mark – a branded triangle inside a circle – upon Mr Douglas's forearm?'

The Valley of Fear

_____

_____

_____

_____

_____

_____

January 29th

'Looking round for my central character I felt that Sherlock Holmes, whom I had already handled in two little books, would easily lend himself to a succession of short stories. These I began in the long hours of waiting in my consulting-room. Greenhough Smith liked them from the first, and encouraged me to go ahead with them. My literary affairs had been taken up by that king of agents, A. P. Watt, who relieved me of all the hateful bargaining, and handled things so well that any immediate anxiety for money soon disappeared.'

Memories and Adventures

_____

_____

_____

_____

_____

_____

_____

_____

_____

January 30th

He disappeared into his bedroom and returned in a
few minutes in the character of an amiable and simple-
minded nonconformist clergyman. His broad black
hat, his baggy trousers, his white tie, his sympathetic
smile and general look of peering and benevolent
curiosity were such as Mr John Hare alone could have
equalled. It was not merely that Holmes changed his
costume. His expression, his manner, his very soul
seemed to vary with every fresh part that he assumed.
The stage lost a fine actor, even as science lost an
acute reasoner, when he became a specialist in crime.

'A Scandal in Bohemia'

_____

_____

_____

_____

_____

_____

_____

January 31st

Through his agent A. P. Watt, Conan Doyle sent *The Strand* a story called 'A Scandal in Bohemia'. Between April and August 1891 he sent off six more stories. And these six were all he intended to write. Greenhough Smith paid his new author £35, less agent's fee, for each story. When 'A Scandal in Bohemia' appeared in the July number of *The Strand*, the reading public responded with wild enthusiasm.

_____

_____

_____

_____

_____

_____

_____

_____

_____

_____

FEBRUARY

The cover of the bound edition of
The Strand Magazine, *January to June 1894,*
designed by George Charles Haité

February 1st

In May 1891 Conan Doyle suffered a life-threatening attack of influenza. On his recovery, he wrote, 'It was then, as I surveyed my own life, that I saw how foolish I was to waste my literary earnings in keeping up an oculist's room in Wimpole Street, and I determined with a wild rush of joy to cut the painter and to trust for ever to my power of writing. I remember in my delight taking the handkerchief which lay upon the coverlet in my enfeebled hand, and tossing it up to the ceiling in my exultation.'

Memories and Adventures

_____

_____

_____

_____

_____

_____

_____

_____

_____

February 2nd

'He was outside the window, Mr Holmes, with his face pressed against the glass. I have told you that I looked out at the night. When I did so, I left the curtains partly open. His figure was framed in this gap. The window came down to the ground and I could see the whole length of it, but it was his face which held my gaze. He was deadly pale – never have I seen a man so white . . . He sprang back when he saw that I was looking at him, and he vanished into the darkness.'

'The Blanched Soldier'

February 3rd

'*The Strand*,' Conan Doyle wrote to his mother on 14
October 1891, 'are simply imploring me to continue
Holmes.' Very much engaged on his 'serious literary
work' (especially his historical novels, *Micah Clarke*,
The White Company, *The Refugees*, etc.), he told
her he would reply that 'if they offer me £50 each,
irrespective of length, I may be induced to reconsider
my refusal. Seems rather high-handed, does it not?'
The magazine agreed to his terms by return of post.

_____

_____

_____

_____

_____

_____

_____

_____

_____

February 4th

Our visitor had no sooner waddled out of the room –
no other verb can describe Mrs Merrilow's method of
progression – than Sherlock Holmes threw himself
with fierce energy upon the pile of commonplace
books in the corner. For a few minutes there was a
constant swish of the leaves, and then with a grunt of
satisfaction he came upon what he sought. So excited
was he that he did not rise, but sat upon the floor like
some strange Buddha, with crossed legs, the huge
books all round him, and one open upon his knees.

'The Veiled Lodger'

February 5th

Conan Doyle found all drawings of Holmes 'very unlike my own original idea of the man. I saw him as very tall – "over 6 feet, but so excessively lean that he seemed considerably taller", said *A Study in Scarlet*. He had, as I imagined him, a thin razor-like face, with a great hawk's-bill of a nose, and two small eyes, set close together on either side of it. Such was my conception. It chanced, however, that poor Sidney Paget, who, before his premature death, drew all the original pictures [for the short stories] had a younger brother whose name, I think, was Walter, who served him as a model. The handsome Walter took the place of the more powerful but uglier Sherlock, and perhaps from the point of view of my lady readers it was as well.' (D. H. Friston and George Hutchinson provided illustrations for *A Study in Scarlet*.)

_____

_____

_____

_____

_____

_____

February 6th

Finally he examined with his glass the word upon the wall, going over every letter of it with the most minute exactness. This done, he appeared to be satisfied, for he replaced his tape and his glass in his pocket.

'They say that genius is an infinite capacity for taking pains,' he remarked with a smile. 'It's a very bad definition, but it does apply to detective work.'

A Study in Scarlet

February 7th

Increasingly ambivalent about his famous creation, in November 1891 Conan Doyle confessed to his mother, 'I am thinking of slaying Holmes . . . and winding him up for good and all. He takes my mind off better things.' She protested, 'You won't! You can't! You mustn't!' But Conan Doyle was not convinced. 'They have been bothering me for more Sherlock Holmes tales,' he complained in February 1892. 'Under pressure, I offered to do a dozen for a thousand pounds, and I sincerely hope they won't accept it.' They did. The resulting series of stories included 'Silver Blaze', 'The Reigate Squires' and 'The Naval Treaty'.

February 8th

I saw by the inspector's face that his attention had been keenly aroused . . .

'Is there any point to which you would wish to draw my attention?'

'To the curious incident of the dog in the night-time.'

'The dog did nothing in the night-time.'

'That was the curious incident,' remarked Sherlock Holmes.

'Silver Blaze'

_____

_____

_____

_____

_____

_____

_____

_____

_____

February 9th

'People have often asked me whether I knew the end of a Holmes story before I started it. Of course I did. One could not possibly steer a course if one did not know one's destination. The first thing is to get your idea. Having got that key idea one's next task is to conceal it and lay emphasis upon everything which can make for a different explanation. Holmes, however, can see all the fallacies of the alternatives, and arrives more or less dramatically at the true solution by steps which he can describe and justify.'

Memories and Adventures

_____

_____

_____

_____

_____

_____

_____

_____

_____

February 10th

'Good heavens, Mr Holmes! What is the matter?'

My poor friend's face had suddenly assumed the most dreadful expression. His eyes rolled upwards, his features writhed in agony, and with a suppressed groan he dropped on his face upon the ground. Horrified at the suddenness and severity of the attack, we carried him into the kitchen, where he lay back in a large chair, and breathed heavily for some minutes. Finally, with a shamefaced apology for his weakness, he rose once more.

'The Reigate Squires'

February 11th

'I do not think that I ever realised what a living actual personality Holmes had become to the more guileless readers, until I heard of the very pleasing story of the charabanc of French schoolboys who, when asked what they wanted to see first in London, replied unanimously that they wanted to see Mr Holmes's lodgings in Baker Street. Many have asked me which house it is, but that is a point which for excellent reasons I will not decide.'

Memories and Adventures

February 12th

Standing on the rug between us, with his slight, tall figure, his sharp features, thoughtful face, and curling hair prematurely tinged with grey, he seemed to represent that not too common type, a nobleman who is in truth noble.

'Your name is very familiar to me, Mr Holmes,' said he, smiling. 'And, of course, I cannot pretend to be ignorant of the object of your visit.'

'The Naval Treaty'

February 13th

'The impression that Holmes was a real person of flesh and blood may have been intensified by his frequent appearance upon the stage. After the withdrawal of my dramatisation of *Rodney Stone* from a theatre upon which I held a six months' lease, I determined to play a bold and energetic game, for an empty theatre spells ruin. When I saw the course that things were taking I shut myself up and devoted my whole mind to making a sensational Sherlock Holmes drama. I wrote it in a week and called it *The Speckled Band* after the short story of that name.'

Memories and Adventures

_____

_____

_____

_____

_____

_____

_____

_____

February 14th

'Ha! I am glad to see that Mrs Hudson has had the good sense to light the fire. Pray draw up to it, and I shall order you a cup of hot coffee, for I observe that you are shivering.'

'It is not cold which makes me shiver,' said the woman in a low voice, changing her seat as requested.

'What, then?'

'It is fear, Mr Holmes. It is terror.' She raised her veil as she spoke . . .

'The Speckled Band'

_____

_____

_____

February 15th

'There are certain Sherlock Holmes stories, apocryphal I need not say, which go round and round the press and turn up at fixed intervals with the regularity of a comet. One is the story of the cabman who is supposed to have taken me to a hotel in Paris. "Dr Doyle," he cried, gazing at me fixedly, "I perceive from your appearance that you have been recently at Constantinople. I have reason to think also that you have been at Buda, and I perceive some indication that you were not far from Milan." "Wonderful. Five francs for the secret of how you did it?" "I looked at the labels pasted on your trunk," said the astute cabby.'

Memories and Adventures

_____

_____

_____

_____

_____

_____

_____

_____

February 16th

Mr Windibank sprang out of his chair and picked up his hat. 'I cannot waste time over this sort of fantastic talk, Mr Holmes,' he said. 'If you can catch the man, catch him, and let me know when you have done it.'

'Certainly,' said Holmes, stepping over and turning the key in the door. 'I let you know, then, that I have caught him!'

'What! where?' shouted Mr Windibank, turning white to his lips and glancing about him like a rat in a trap.

'A Case of Identity'

February 17th

'Another perennial is of the woman who is said to have consulted Sherlock. "I am greatly puzzled, sir. In one week I have lost a motor horn, a brush, a box of golf balls, a dictionary and a bootjack. Can you explain it?" "Nothing simpler, madame," said Sherlock. "It is clear that your neighbour keeps a goat."

'There was a third about how Sherlock entered heaven, and by virtue of his power of observation at once greeted Adam, but the point is perhaps too anatomical for further discussion.'

Memories and Adventures

_____

_____

_____

_____

_____

_____

_____

_____

_____

February 18th

The servant who had first entered had thrown up the window, or it would have been even more intolerable. This might partly be due to the fact that a lamp stood flaring and smoking on the centre table. Beside it sat the dead man, leaning back in his chair, his thin beard projecting, his spectacles pushed up on to his forehead, and his lean dark face turned towards the window and twisted into the same distortion of terror which had marked the features of his dead sister. His limbs were convulsed and his fingers contorted as though he had died in a very paroxysm of fear.

'The Devil's Foot'

February 19th

Conan Doyle's marriage to Louise was a source of happiness and support during his rise to fame. Their daughter, Marie Louise, was born (delivered by her father) in Southsea in 1889 and their son, Alleyne Kingsley, at their new house, 12 Tennison Road, South Norwood, in 1892. Sadly, little more than a year later, Louise was found to be suffering from tuberculosis and the family travelled to Switzerland where her husband hoped the climate would help to arrest the progress of the disease.

_____

_____

_____

_____

_____

_____

_____

_____

_____

February 20th

It was that vision which gave me an instant of sanity and of strength. I dashed from my chair, threw my arms round Holmes, and together we lurched through the door, and an instant afterwards had thrown ourselves down upon the grass plot and were lying side by side, conscious only of the glorious sunshine which was bursting its way through the hellish cloud of terror which had girt us in. Slowly it rose from our souls like the mists from a landscape until peace and reason had returned, and we were sitting upon the grass . . .

'The Devil's Foot'

_____

_____
_____

_____
_____
_____
_____
_____
_____

February 21st

It was during this period that Conan Doyle became the first Englishman to cross an Alpine pass in snow shoes. Furthermore, it was he who introduced skiing as a sport into Switzerland. 'You don't appreciate it as yet,' he told fellow guests at the hotel where the family was staying, 'but the time will come when hundreds of Englishmen will come to Switzerland for the skiing season.' He was a man who loved physical pursuits and prided himself on being an all-round sportsman.

_____

_____

_____

_____

_____

_____

_____

_____

February 22nd

'Farewell, then,' said the old man solemnly. 'Your own deathbeds, when they come, will be the easier for the thought of the peace which you have given to mine.' Tottering and shaking in all his giant frame, he stumbled slowly from the room.

'God help us!' said Holmes after a long silence. 'Why does fate play such tricks with poor, helpless worms? I never hear of such a case as this that I do not think of Baxter's words, and say, "There, but for the grace of God, goes Sherlock Holmes." '

'The Boscombe Valley Mystery'

_____

_____

_____

_____   _____

February 23rd

Conan Doyle's father Charles, a complex and tormented character, died suddenly in October 1893, in Crichton Royal Institution in Dumfries. Conan Doyle had come to understand his father better in adulthood; to please him he had cherished a plan to collect together his paintings and arrange an exhibition of them in London – but now it was too late. His mother, on the other hand, was very much alive, and she was his indispensable confidante. He wrote to her about everything, and more than a thousand of his letters, from when he was a boy away at school up until her death in 1920, survive.

_____

_____

_____

_____

_____

_____

_____

_____

February 24th

'Well, to come to an end of the matter, Mr Holmes, and not to abuse your patience, there came a night when he made one of those drunken sallies but this time never came back. We found him, when we went to search for him, face downward in a little green-scummed pool, which lay at the foot of the garden. There was no sign of any violence, and the water was but two feet deep, so that the jury, having regard to his known eccentricity, brought in a verdict of suicide.'

'The Five Orange Pips'

_____

_____

_____

_____

_____

_____

_____

_____

_____

_____

February 25th

During a visit to the Reichenbach Falls in Switzerland early in 1893, a visit made in a bid to recover from the exhaustion of plot-spinning, Conan Doyle hardened his resolve. He wrote to his mother immediately on his return to Norwood, 'All is well down here. I am in the middle of the last Holmes story, after which the gentleman vanishes, never to return! I am weary of his name.'

_____

_____

_____

_____

_____

_____

_____

_____

_____

February 26th

Outside the wind still screamed and the rain splashed and pattered against the windows. This strange, wild story seemed to have come to us from amid the mad elements – blown in upon us like a sheet of seaweed in a gale – and now to have been reabsorbed by them once more.

Sherlock Holmes sat for some time in silence . . . 'I think, Watson,' he remarked at last, 'that of all our cases we have had none more fantastic than this.'

'The Five Orange Pips'

February 27th

'All [my other] books had some decent success, though none of it was remarkable. It was still the Sherlock Holmes stories for which the public clamoured, and these from time to time I endeavoured to supply. At last, after I had done two series of them, I saw that I was in danger of having my hand forced, and of being entirely identified with what I regarded as a lower stratum of literary achievement. Therefore as a sign of my resolution I determined to end the life of my hero. The idea was in my mind when I went with my wife for a short holiday in Switzerland, in the course of which we saw there the wonderful falls of Reichenbach, a terrible place, and one that I thought would make a worthy tomb for poor Sherlock, even if I buried my banking account along with him. So there I laid him, fully determined that he should stay there – as indeed for some years he did.'

Memories and Adventures

February 28th

A few words may suffice to tell the little that remains. An examination by experts leaves little doubt that a personal contest between the two men ended, as it could hardly fail to end in such a situation, in their reeling over, locked in each other's arms. Any attempt at recovering the bodies was absolutely hopeless, and there, deep down in that dreadful cauldron of swirling water and seething foam, will lie for all time the most dangerous criminal and the foremost champion of the law of their generation.

_____

_____

_____

_____

_____

_____

_____

_____

February 29th

Being out of England, Conan Doyle did not hear the clamour which arose from his grief-stricken readers when they opened their copies of *The Strand* in December 1893 and learned of the death of their hero. Young clerks went to their offices in the City with crape bands round their hats as a sign of mourning for the incomparable Sherlock Holmes. When the guilty author brought his wife and children back to their bereft country, via Italy and Egypt, it was to the splendid home he had built for them, Undershaw, in Surrey.

_____

_____

_____

_____

_____

_____

_____

_____

_____

MARCH

March 1st

'I was amazed at the concern expressed by the public. They say that a man is never properly appreciated until he is dead, and the general protest against my summary execution of Holmes taught me how devoted and how numerous were his friends. "You Brute" was the beginning of the letter of remonstrance which one lady sent me, and I expect she spoke for others besides herself. I heard of many who wept. I fear I was utterly callous myself, and only glad to have a chance of opening out into new fields of imagination, for the temptation of high prices made it difficult to get one's thoughts away from Holmes.'

Memories and Adventures

March 2nd

As I passed the tall man who sat by the brazier I felt a sudden pluck at my sleeve, and a low voice whispered, 'Walk past me, and then look back at me.' I took two steps forward and looked back . . . and there, sitting by the fire and grinning at my surprise, was none other than Sherlock Holmes . . . He made a slight motion to me to approach him, and instantly, as he turned his face half round to the company once more, subsided into a doddering, loose-lipped senility.

'Holmes!' I whispered, 'what on earth are you doing in this den?'

'The Man with the Twisted Lip'

March 3rd

The Doyles lived at Undershaw from 1897 to 1907. The Surrey house, situated at Hindhead, the highest point of the county, and specially adapted to his wife's needs, became a place of pilgrimage for Conan Doyle's admirers. It was there he wrote *The Hound of the Baskervilles* and it was there he entertained most of the major figures of the day.

_____

_____

_____

_____

_____

_____

_____

_____

_____

_____

March 4th

We all three shook hands, and I saw at once, from the reverential way in which Lestrade gazed at my companion, that he had learned a good deal since the days when they had first worked together. I could well remember the scorn which the theories of the reasoner used then to excite in the practical man.

'Anything good?' he asked.

'The biggest thing for years,' said Holmes.

The Hound of the Baskervilles

March 5th

Conan Doyle was determined to challenge the gloomy prognosis meted out to his stricken wife: 'And we succeeded. When I think that the attack was one of what is called "galloping consumption", and that the doctors did not give more than a few months, and yet that we postponed the fatal issue from 1893 to 1906, I think it is proof that the successive measures were wise. The invalid's life was happy too, for it was necessarily spent in glorious scenery. It was seldom marred by pain, and it was sustained by that optimism which is peculiar to the disease, and which came naturally to her quietly contented nature.'

_____

_____

_____

_____

_____

_____

_____

_____

March 6th

' "My accomplishments, sir, may be less than you image," said I. "A little French, a little German, music and drawing – "

' "Tut, tut!" he cried. "This is all quite beside the question. The point is, have you or have you not the bearing and deportment of a lady?" '

'The Copper Beeches'

March 7th

On 15 March 1897, the year of Queen Victoria's Diamond Jubilee, Conan Doyle, at the age of thirty-eight, met and fell in love with Jean Leckie, an accomplished twenty-four-year-old who possessed beauty, breeding, musical talent and a calculating mind. She returned his love and their passionate relationship lasted until his death. The conflicted husband confided to his mother : '[Touie] is as dear to me as ever, but there is a large side of my life which was unoccupied but is no longer so.' The couple conducted a discreet affair until Touie's death in 1906 left them free to marry. The marriage which took place on 18 September 1907 was one to which she had given her blessing.

_____

_____

_____

_____

_____

_____

_____

March 8th

'See here, sir! See what my wife found in its crop!'

He held out his hand and displayed upon the centre of the palm a brilliantly scintillating blue stone, rather smaller than a bean in size, but of such purity and radiance that it twinkled like an electric point in the dark hollow of his hand.

'The Blue Carbuncle'

_____

_____

_____

_____

_____

March 9th

When, in 1901, Conan Doyle returned to Undershaw from South Africa, where he had been working as a volunteer physician at the Langman Field Hospital in Bloemfontein during the Second Boer War, he had not written about Sherlock Holmes for eight years. Having had Holmes and Professor Moriarty plunge to their deaths in the Reichenbach Falls in the notorious last story 'The Final Problem', he was now in something of a quandary. Funding his lifestyle – he had taken up hunting and other expensive pursuits and was thinking of standing for Parliament – was financially demanding and he was forever being reminded that the public's appetite for Holmes had never gone away.

_____

_____

_____

_____

_____

_____

_____

_____

March 10th

'He is the Napoleon of crime, Watson. He is the organiser of half that is evil and of nearly all that is undetected in this great city. He is a genius, a philosopher, an abstract thinker. He has a brain of the first order. He sits motionless, like a spider in the centre of its web, but that web has a thousand radiations, and he knows well every quiver of each of them.'

'The Final Problem'

March 11th

On a windswept golfing holiday at the Royal Links Hotel in Cromer, Conan Doyle and his friend Fletcher Robinson discussed the legends of Dartmoor and especially the story of a spectral hound. Conan Doyle had used the idea of such a beast in 'The King of the Foxes' in 1898, but he had never used the gothic unearthliness of Dartmoor as a backdrop for any of his stories, having never visited the desolate place. Now he wrote to his mother that he was planning a 'little book' called *The Hound of the Baskervilles*. 'A real Creeper!'

March 12th

March 13th

On 2 April 1901, Conan Doyle wrote from Rowe's Duchy Hotel, Princetown, Dartmoor, Devon: 'Here I am in the highest town in England. Robinson and I are exploring the Moor over our Sherlock Holmes book. I think it will work out splendidly: indeed I have already done nearly half of it. Holmes is at his very best, and it is a highly dramatic idea – which I owe to Robinson.'

_____

_____

_____

_____

_____

_____

_____

_____

_____

_____

March 14th

'You know the story of the hound?'

'I do not believe in such nonsense.'

'But I do. If you have any influence with Sir Henry, take him away from a place which has always been fatal to his family. The world is wide. Why should he wish to live at the place of danger?'

The Hound of the Baskervilles

March 15th

At first it did not occur to Conan Doyle to cast Sherlock Holmes as the detecting genius destined to unravel the mystery of the ghostly hound. As the plot developed, however, he asked himself, 'Why should I invent such a character when I have him already in the form of Holmes?' When Sir George Newnes, the proprietor of *The Strand Magazine*, reported there was at last to be another story, the news was greeted with great rejoicing among the staff and the shareholders, but they and their millions of readers were disappointed when they heard that the adventure was to be set *before* Holmes's demise. 'He is at the foot of the Reichenbach Falls,' insisted Conan Doyle, 'and there he stays!'

March 16th

The light shone steadily as if he were standing motionless. I crept down the passage as noiselessly as I could and peeped round the corner of the door.

Barrymore was crouching at the window with the candle held against the glass. His profile was half turned towards me, and his face seemed to be rigid with expectation as he stared out into the blackness of the moor.

The Hound of the Baskervilles

March 17th

The third of the four full-length novels featuring Sherlock Holmes, *The Hound of the Baskervilles* was first published in *The Strand Magazine* in nine instalments, from August 1901 to April 1902. Each episode ended in a cliff-hanger, leaving the reader impatient for the next instalment. One year later the novel was published in book form and from that day to this it has never been out of print. It is the most famous of Sherlock Holmes's adventures and has been adapted for radio, stage and screen many times.

_____

_____

_____

_____

_____

_____

_____

_____

_____

March 18th

'Did you correspond with him?'

The lady looked quickly up with an angry gleam in her hazel eyes. 'What is the object of these questions?' she asked sharply.

'The object is to avoid a public scandal. It is better that I should ask them here than that the matter should pass outside our control.'

She was silent and her face was still very pale. At last she looked up with something reckless and defiant in her manner. 'Well, I'll answer,' she said. 'What are your questions?'

The Hound of the Baskervilles

March 19th

In 1902, the individual pages of the original manuscript of *The Hound of the Baskervilles* were distributed
by Conan Doyle's American publisher to booksellers
to be used in promotional window displays. Out of
the estimated 185 pages only 36 are known still to
exist, among them the whole of Chapter 11 which is
held by New York Public Library. Other pages are
owned by university libraries and private collectors. A
page which came to light in 2012 was sold at auction
for $158,500.

March 20th

'And now, my dear Watson, we have had some weeks of severe work, and for one evening, I think, we may turn our thoughts into more pleasant channels. I have a box for *Les Huguenots* . . . Might I trouble you then to be ready in half an hour, and we can stop at Marcini's for a little dinner on the way?'

The Hound of the Baskervilles

_____

_____

_____

_____

_____

_____

_____

_____

_____

March 21st

When American theatrical producer Charles Frohman approached Conan Doyle for the stage rights to Sherlock Holmes, the author, who had always had an interest in writing for the stage, offered him a five-act play he had written himself. Frohman persuaded him to collaborate on a rewrite with the actor William Gillette, who was not only a successful playwright but would also make an ideal Sherlock Holmes. The play, which drew on material from several of the stories, opened in New York City on 6 November 1899. It ran there for 260 performances and then toured the United States before opening at London's Lyceum Theatre in September 1901. Gillette revived the play in 1905, 1906, 1910 and 1915.

March 22nd

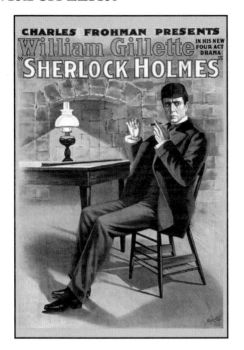

March 23rd

At first, Conan Doyle was uneasy about William Gillette's adaptation of his work for the stage, but when he saw *Sherlock Holmes* he declared himself 'charmed by the play, the acting and the pecuniary result'. When Gillette cabled asking, 'May I marry Holmes?' Conan Doyle replied, 'You may marry him, murder him, or do anything you like to him!' Among the changes he made, Gillette developed an unnamed pageboy from 'A Case of Identity' into a character called Billy whom Conan Doyle himself used in later stories and who was played on the stage by a thirteen-year-old Charlie Chaplin. Gillette was responsible for the phrase, 'Elementary, my dear Watson,' and it was he who introduced the famous curved pipe as a trademark Holmes prop.

_____

_____

_____

_____

_____

_____

_____

March 24th

'A house on fire?' asked Bradstreet . . .

'Whose house is it?'

'Dr Becher's.'

'Tell me,' broke in the engineer, 'is Dr Becher a German, very thin, with a long, sharp nose?'

The station-master laughed heartily. 'No, sir, Dr Becher is an Englishman, and there isn't a man in the parish who has a better-lined waistcoat. But he has a gentleman staying with him, a patient, as I understand, who is a foreigner, and he looks as if a little good Berkshire beef would do him no harm.'

'The Engineer's Thumb'

_____

_____

_____

_____

_____

_____

_____

_____

_____

March 25th

Conan Doyle was an enthusiastic amateur sportsman. As a young doctor in Southsea, under the name of A. C. Smith, he had been goalkeeper for Portsmouth Association Football Club, the precursor of today's Portsmouth FC. Between 1899 and 1907 he played for the Marylebone Cricket Club (MCC), and on one famous occasion bowled out W. G. Grace. He belonged to the Allahackberries, an amateur cricket team whose members included J. M. Barrie and A. A. Milne. In 1910 he was elected captain of the Crowborough Beacon Golf Club.

March 26th

The light flashed upon the barrel of a revolver, but Holmes's hunting-crop came down on the man's wrist and the pistol clinked upon the stone floor.

'It's no use, John Clay,' said Holmes blandly. 'You have no chance at all.'

'The Red-Headed League'

March 27th

'Sir James Barrie paid his respects to Sherlock Holmes in a rollicking parody. It was really a gay gesture of resignation over the failure which we had encountered with a comic opera for which he undertook to write the libretto. I collaborated with him on this, but in spite of our joint efforts, the piece fell flat. Whereupon Barrie sent me a parody on Holmes, written on the fly leaves of one of his books. This parody ['The Adventure of the Two Collaborators'], the best of all the numerous parodies, may be taken as an example not only of the author's wit but of his debonair courage, for it was written immediately after our joint failure which at the moment was a bitter thought for both of us. There is indeed nothing more miserable than a theatrical failure, for you feel how many others who have backed you have been affected by it.'

Memories and Adventures

March 28th

'Then perhaps you will kindly explain how it is that
we found this in it?' He opened his bag as he spoke,
and tumbled on to the floor a wedding-dress of
watered silk, a pair of white satin shoes and a bride's
wreath and veil, all discoloured and soaked in water.
'There,' said he, putting a new wedding-ring upon
the top of the pile. 'There is a little nut for you to
crack, Master Holmes.'

'The Noble Bachelor'

_____

_____

_____

_____

97

March 29th

A great fan of boxing, Conan Doyle may have said it was his favourite sport. His interest gave rise to a historical novel in 1896, *Rodney Stone*, about bare-knuckle fighting in the Regency period. It was upon this book that he based his play *The House of Temperley*. The play was a flop (partly because the death of the King temporarily closed the theatre) and he was so busy replacing the play with his adaptation for the stage of 'The Speckled Band', in order to avoid severe financial loss, that he had to turn down an offer from American promoter Ted Rickard to referee a high-profile fight in the United States.

_____

_____

_____

_____

_____

_____

_____

_____

March 30th

'We had got as far as this when who should walk in but the gentleman himself, who had been drinking his beer in the taproom and had heard the whole conversation. Who was I? What did I want? What did I mean by asking questions? He had a fine flow of language, and his adjectives were very vigorous. He ended a string of abuse by a vicious backhander which I failed entirely to avoid. The next few minutes were delicious. It was a straight left against a slogging ruffian. I emerged as you see me. Mr Woodley went home in a cart.'

'The Solitary Cyclist'

March 31st

Following criticism of Britain's role in the Boer War, Conan Doyle leapt to the defence of British policy in *The War in South Africa: Its Cause and Conduct*. It was possibly partly as a result of such uncompromising tokens of his passionate patriotism that he was knighted by Edward VII in 1902 and also that he was appointed Deputy-Lieutenant of Surrey. In 1900, during the time that as a medical volunteer he was out in South Africa, he wrote *The Great Boer War*.

APRIL

THE RETURN OF
Sherlock Holmes
A CONAN DOYLE

April 1st

At first Conan Doyle had no intention of accepting a knighthood. 'It is a silently understood thing in this world that the big men – outside diplomacy and the army, where it is a sort of professional badge – do not condescend to such things. Not that I am a big man, but something inside me revolts at the thought. Fancy Rhodes or Chamberlain or Kipling doing such a thing! And why should my standards be lower than theirs? . . . All my work for the state would be tainted if I took a so-called "reward".' When his mother remonstrated with him, he replied: 'I tell you it is unthinkable. Let us drop the subject.' He was at last persuaded when she told him that his refusal would be an insult to the King.

_____

_____

_____

_____

_____

_____

_____

April 2nd

From the top of this boulder the gleam of something bright caught my eye, and, raising my hand, I found that it came from the silver cigarette-case which he used to carry. As I took it up a small square of paper upon which it had lain fluttered down on to the ground. Unfolding it, I found that it consisted of three pages torn from his notebook and addressed to me. It was characteristic of the man that the direction was as precise, and the writing as firm and clear, as though it had been written in his study.

'The Final Problem'

April 3rd

The shadow of Sherlock Holmes fell across the pleasure Conan Doyle took in the messages of congratulation showered upon him following his visit to the palace. When he received a parcel of shirts addressed to 'Sir Sherlock Holmes' he was not amused. He did not consider his invention worthy of any sort of honour. He must have sighed when, in the spring of 1902, his American publishers wrote to say that if he would find a way to bring Holmes back to life they would pay five thousand dollars a story for as many as he cared to write. His agent assured him that George Newnes would offer more than half as much for the English rights, and begged him to agree. On a postcard Conan Doyle replied: 'Very well. A. C. D.'

_____

_____

_____

_____

_____

_____

_____

April 4th

I withdrew . . . in some disgust. As I did so I struck against an elderly deformed man, who had been behind me, and I knocked down several books which he was carrying. I remember that as I picked them up I observed the title of one of them, *The Origin of Tree Worship*, and it struck me that the fellow must be some poor bibliophile who, either as a trade or as a hobby, was a collector of obscure volumes.

'The Empty House'

April 5th

'I have not done any Holmes stories for seven or eight years [in fact, it was ten] and I don't see why I should not have another go at them . . . I might add that I have finished the first one, called "The Adventure of the Empty House". The plot, by the way, was given to me by Jean, and it is a rare good one. You will find that Holmes was never dead, and that now he is very much alive.' It seemed that only Moriarty had fallen to his death at the Reichenbach Falls. Holmes, beset by dangerous enemies, like Colonel Sebastian Moran, had found it convenient to be perceived to be dead in order to disappear for a while.

_____

_____

_____

_____

_____

_____

_____

_____

_____

April 6th

The fierce old man said nothing, but still glared at my companion; with his savage eyes and bristling moustache he was wonderfully like a tiger himself.

'I wonder that my very simple stratagem could deceive so old a shikari,' said Holmes . . .

Colonel Moran sprang forward, with a snarl of rage, but the constables dragged him back. The fury upon his face was terrible to look at.

'The Empty House'

April 7th

The first if the thirteen stories comprising *The Return of Sherlock Homes* appeared in *The Strand* in October 1903. 'The scenes at the railway-bookstalls,' remembered a lady shopper, 'were worse than anything I ever saw at a bargain-sale. My husband, when he was drunk, used to recite to me pages from *A Duet*, but I could never see anything in that. Holmes was a different matter.' The *Westminster Gazette* reported: 'It is as we suspected. That fall over the cliff did not kill Holmes. In fact, he never fell at all. He climbed up the other side of the cliff to avoid his enemies, and churlishly left poor Watson in ignorance. We call this mean. All the same, who can complain?'

_____

_____

_____

_____

_____

_____

_____

_____

April 8th

She rummaged in a bureau, and presently she produced a photograph of a woman, shamefully defaced and mutilated with a knife. 'That is my own photograph,' she said. 'He sent it to me in that state, with his curse, upon my wedding morning.'

'Well,' said I, 'at least he has forgiven you now, since he has left all his property to your son.'

'Neither my son nor I want anything from Jonas Oldacre, dead or alive,' she cried, with a proper spirit.

'The Norwood Builder'

April 9th

Sidney Edward Paget was born in Clerkenwell in London in 1860 and was trained at the Royal Academy Schools as a painter and illustrator. He was gifted and prolific. His paintings were exhibited and his illustrative work appeared in the *Pictorial World*, the *Sphere*, the *Graphic*, the *Illustrated London News* and the *Pall Mall Gazette*, but it was his association with *The Strand Magazine* that made him famous. He was commissioned to illustrate the stories they were running about a charismatic new detective, Sherlock Holmes, and he worked on all the stories up to the Reichenbach Falls. When Conan Doyle revived Holmes he asked most specifically for Paget to continue as his illustrator.

April 10th

For a moment I wished that I were armed. Sterndale's fierce face turned to a dusky red, his eyes glared, and the knotted, passionate veins started out in his forehead, while he sprang forward with clenched hands towards my companion. Then he stopped, and with a violent effort he resumed a cold, rigid calmness, which was, perhaps, more suggestive of danger than his hotheaded outburst.

'I have lived so long among savages and beyond the law,' said he, 'that I have got into the way of being a law to myself.'

'The Devil's Foot'

_____

_____

_____

_____

_____

_____

_____

_____

_____

April 11th

It was Sidney Paget who created the universally recognised image of Sherlock Holmes. The deerstalker cap and Inverness cape were his own inspired inventions. He is said to have modelled Dr Watson on a friend from student days, Alfred Morris Butler. In all, he illustrated one of the four novels and thirty-seven of the short stories. His indelible images have fixed the appearance of the detective in fiction and, more widely, on stage and screen. His distinctive style has influenced American detective movies and film noir and made an icon of Holmes.

_____

_____

_____

_____

_____

_____

_____

_____

_____

April 12th

'Good heavens!' I cried. 'Who would associate crime with these dear old homesteads?'

'They always fill me with a certain horror. It is my belief, Watson, founded upon my experience, that the lowest and vilest alleys in London do not present a more dreadful record of sin than does the smiling and beautiful countryside.'

'The Copper Beeches'

April 13th

Holmes's famous portrayer died in Margate in January 1908 of a chronic chest complaint. He was only forty-seven. In total, he had made 356 drawings of his immortal subject. A complete set of *The Strand Magazine* featuring the stories is the rarest and most expensive collector's item in publishing history. Paget's original drawing of 'Holmes and Moriarty in Mortal Combat on the Edge of the Reichenbach Falls' was sold at Sotheby's in New York in 2004 for $220,800. The two-handed clasp that Holmes used on Moriarty in that scene was depicted in the 2011 film *Sherlock Holmes: A Game of Shadows*, although Conan Doyle himself made no mention of it.

April 14th

'I've no time to talk to every gadabout. We want no stranger here. Be off, or you may find a dog at your heels.'

Holmes leaned forward and whispered something in the trainer's ear. He started violently and flushed to the temples.

'It's a lie!' he shouted, 'an infernal lie!'

'Very good. Shall we argue about it here in public or talk it over in your parlour?'

'Silver Blaze'

April 15th

Having written the thirteen stories of *The Return of Sherlock Holmes* in one energetic spurt, Conan Doyle resumed work on his many other projects, especially the literary tasks so much closer to his heart. Keenly interested in all new inventions, he was characteristically enthused by the rapid developments in transport technology. By 1906 there were two motor cars and a Roc motorcycle in the stables at Undershaw. When asked by a reporter, 'Can we expect to hear of the famous detective hunting down his quarry on the newest and finest type of motorcycle,' he replied, 'No! In Holmes's early days motor-bicycles were unheard of. Besides, Holmes has now retired into private life.'

_____

_____

_____

_____

_____

_____

_____

April 16th

Holmes, however, was always in training, for he had inexhaustible stores of nervous energy upon which to draw. His springy step never slowed until suddenly, when he was a hundred yards in front of me, he halted, and I saw him throw up his hand with a gesture of grief and despair. At the same instant an empty dog-cart, the horse cantering, the reins trailing, appeared round the curve of the road and rattled swiftly towards us.

'Too late, Watson; too late!' cried Holmes, as I ran panting to his side. 'Fool that I was not to allow for that earlier train! It's abduction, Watson – abduction! Murder! Heaven knows what! Block the road! Stop the horse!'

'The Solitary Cyclist'

April 17th

'Holmes could never die again. He could only retire; he was for ever condemned to life,' in the words of John Dickson Carr. Conan Doyle's wife Louise, however, was dying. 'It may be days,' he wrote to his brother Innes, 'or it may be weeks, but the end now seems inevitable. She is without pain in body, and easy in mind, taking it all with her usual sweet and gentle equanimity.' In the press on 5 July 1906 appeared a brief paragraph: 'Lady Conan Doyle, the wife of Sir Arthur Conan Doyle the novelist, died at three o'clock yesterday morning at Undershaw, Hindhead. The deceased lady, who was forty-nine years of age, had been in delicate health for some years.'

_____

_____

_____

_____

_____

_____

_____

_____

April 18th

On the bed a woman was lying who was clearly in a high fever. She was only half conscious, but as I entered she raised a pair of frightened but beautiful eyes and glared at me in apprehension. Seeing a stranger, she appeared to be relieved, and sank back with a sigh upon the pillow. I stepped up to her with a few reassuring words, and she lay still while I took her pulse and temperature. Both were high, and yet my impression was that the condition was rather that of mental and nervous excitement than of any actual seizure.

'The Sussex Vampire'

April 19th

In the period of grief that followed Louise's death, Conan Doyle assumed the mantle of his great protagonist and involved himself in two criminal cases in which he considered there had been miscarriages of justice: that of George Edalji and that of Oscar Slater. His intervention led to both men being exonerated. Conan Doyle's campaigning convinced the legal profession that a better mechanism for reviewing unsafe verdicts was called for, and it was partly as a result of his efforts that the Court of Criminal Appeal was established in 1907.

_____

_____

_____

_____

_____

_____

_____

_____

_____

April 20th

'Pipes are occasionally of extraordinary interest,' said he. 'Nothing has more individuality, save perhaps watches and bootlaces. The indications here, however, are neither very marked nor very important. The owner is obviously a muscular man, left-handed, with an excellent set of teeth, careless in his habits, and with no need to practise economy.' . . .

'You think a man must be well-to-do if he smokes a seven-shilling pipe,' said I.

'This is Grosvenor mixture at eightpence an ounce,' Holmes answered, knocking a little out on his palm. 'As he might get an excellent smoke for half the price, he has no need to practise economy.'

'The Yellow Face'

_____

_____

_____

_____

_____

_____

_____

April 21st

'George Edalji,' wrote Conan Doyle, 'was a young law student, son of the Reverend S. Edalji, the Parsee vicar of the parish of Great Wyrley, who had married an English lady. How the vicar came to be a Parsee, or how the Parsee came to be the vicar, I have no idea. Perhaps some catholic-minded parson wished to demonstrate the universality of the Anglican Church. The experiment will not, I hope, be repeated, for though the vicar was an amiable and devoted man, the appearance of a coloured clergyman with a half-cast son in a rude, unrefined parish was bound to cause some regrettable situation.' Once apprised of the details of the 'regrettable situation' which had arisen, Conan Doyle charged into battle on Edalji's behalf.

_____

_____

_____

_____

_____

_____

_____

April 22nd

'The real murderer is standing immediately behind you.' He stepped past and laid his hand upon the glossy neck of the thoroughbred.

'The horse!' cried both the colonel and myself.

'Yes, the horse . . . But there goes the bell, and as I stand to win a little on this next race, I shall defer a lengthy explanation until a more fitting time.'

'Silver Blaze'

April 23rd

Edalji had been sentenced to seven years' hard labour in 1903 for the brutal maiming of a horse. He was accused of mutilating other animals and writing threatening letters. Alerted to the highly unusual nature of this complex case, Conan Doyle examined every scrap of information he could find. Within months he had proved that the young man had been convicted on grossly flawed evidence and revealed the identity of the culprit. Edajli was released late in 1906 and granted a pardon for the maiming conviction in 1907.

April 24th

' "No, no, Jack, for God's sake!" she gasped, in uncontrollable emotion. Then, as I approached the door, she seized my sleeve and pulled me back with convulsive strength. "I implore you not to do this, Jack," she cried. "I swear that I will tell you everything some day, but nothing but misery can come of it if you enter that cottage . . . " '

'The Yellow Face'

_____

_____

_____

_____

_____

_____

_____

_____

_____

_____

April 25th

'Sherlock Holmes quietly married,' reported the *Buenos Aires Standard*, describing a very private ceremony one afternoon at St Margaret's, Westminster. A Belgian correspondent told his readers: 'Conan Doyle, the English writer who invented the English type of detective, Sherlock Holmes, has just been married.' A French journalist tells us that 'the young lady was enthralled into marriage by the extraordinary adventures of the king of detectives'. The two set off afterwards on a cruise through the eastern Mediterranean. On their return they moved into Windlesham, a house near her family in Crowborough, Sussex. 'As I paid for it with a sum of money which I recovered after I had been unjustly defrauded of it, my friends suggested "Swindlesham" as a more appropriate name,' quipped the jovial bridegroom.

_____

_____

_____

_____

_____

_____

April 26th

'In that case the coincidence must indeed be an extraordinary one. But I think that we shall succeed in establishing a connection, after all. I wish to be perfectly frank with you, Mrs Lyons. We regard this case as one of murder, and the evidence may implicate not only your friend Mr Stapleton but his wife as well.'

The lady sprang from her chair.

'His wife!' she cried.

'The fact is no longer a secret. The person who has passed for his sister is really his wife.'

The Hound of the Baskervilles

_____

_____

_____

_____

_____

_____

_____

_____

_____

April 27th

'On 18 September 1907,' Conan Doyle wrote many years later, 'I married Miss Jean Leckie, the younger daughter of a Blackheath family whom I had known for years, and who was a dear friend of my mother and sister. There are some things which one feels too intimately to be able to express, and I can only say that the years have passed without one shadow coming to mar even for a moment the sunshine of my Indian summer which now deepens to a golden autumn. She and my three younger children with the kindly sympathy of my two elder ones have made my home an ideally happy one.' Every year on their anniversary he presented her with a single snowdrop.

April 28th

'Yes, sir. And no later than this morning. I went to my work as usual at ten o'clock, but the door was shut and locked, with a little square of cardboard hammered on to the middle of the panel with a tack. Here it is, and you can read for yourself.'

He held up a piece of white cardboard about the size of a sheet of notepaper. It read in this fashion:

The Red-Headed League is Dissolved
9 October 1890

_____

_____

_____

_____

_____

_____

_____

_____

_____

_____

April 29th

In truth, Mary and Kingsley, his children by Louise, felt rather cut out after the marriage. Mary complained to her brother, 'I can't think why my father is so hard. I have not had one gentle word or sign of love from him during the whole two years since mother died.' Against her will, Mary was sent to Dresden to study music and discouraged from coming home at times like Christmas. An accomplished singer, she was told by her father that her voice had 'a sweet quality but can never stand out from others'. Mary was probably right to suspect that he was being influenced by the jealousy if her stepmother, a trained mezzo soprano.

_____

_____

_____

_____

_____

_____

_____

_____

April 30th

'Well, we may save the police some little trouble in that direction,' said Holmes, glancing at the haggard figure huddled up by the window. 'Human nature is a strange mixture, Watson. You see that even a villain and murderer can inspire such affection that his brother turns to suicide when he learns that his neck is forfeited.'

'The Stockbroker's Clerk'

_____

_____

_____

_____

_____

MAY

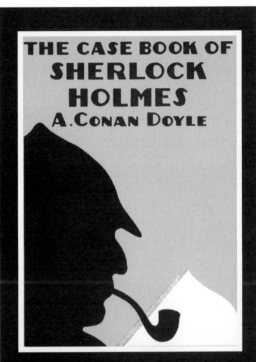

May 1st

Then suddenly another sound became audible – a very gentle, soothing sound, like that of a small jet of steam escaping continually from a kettle. The instant that we heard it, Holmes sprang from the bed, struck a match and lashed furiously with his cane at the bell-pull.

'The Speckled Band'

_____

_____

_____

_____

_____

May 2nd

In 1910, Conan Doyle devoted himself to the case of a German Jew named Oscar Slater who had been falsely convicted of murder. Two years earlier, a Glasgow resident, a Miss Gilchrist, had been violently killed in her flat while her servant-maid was absent on an errand. Robbery did not appear to be the motive, though a diamond brooch may have been missing. Although Slater was 'a gambler and adventurer of uncertain morals and dubious ways', Conan Doyle was convinced of his innocence. Fellow campaigners were Marshall Hall and Ramsay MacDonald. Slater spent eighteen years in prison before being suddenly released. Eventually his conviction was quashed in July 1928 and he received £6,000 in compensation.

_____

_____

_____

_____

_____

_____

_____

May 3rd

Then we rushed on into the captain's cabin, but as we pushed open the door there was an explosion from within, and there he lay with his brains smeared over the chart of the Atlantic which was pinned upon the table, while the chaplain stood with a smoking pistol in his hand at his elbow. The two mates had both been seized by the crew, and the whole business seemed to be settled.

'The *Gloria Scott*'

May 4th

The years from 1907 until the outbreak of war in 1914 were perhaps the happiest of Conan Doyle's life. Windlesham was transformed from a modest country house into an impressive mansion, usually overflowing with guests. Among them were not only the lions of the literary world, like Kipling, but sportsmen, politicians, actors, explorers . . . The American detective William J. Burns brought news of the 'Detectaphone' and (like everyone else) plied him with questions about Sherlock Holmes. In March 1909, Jean gave birth to their first son, Denis Percy Stewart.

May 5th

'Well, gentlemen,' he asked, 'what can I do for you?'

'We came,' I explained, 'in answer to your wire.'

'My wire! I sent no wire.'

'I mean the wire which you sent to Mr Josiah Amberley about his wife and his money.'

'If this is a joke, sir, it is a very questionable one,' said the vicar angrily. 'I have never heard of the gentleman you name, and I have not sent a wire to anyone.'

'The Retired Colourman'

_____

_____

May 6th

In the early days of his second marriage, to please Jean, Conan Doyle wrote two new Sherlock Holmes stories, 'Wisteria Lodge' and 'The Bruce-Partington Plans'. In his bulging daily postbag there were often letters from readers begging him to help them solve cases they were caught up in. For instance, the relatives of a Polish nobleman under suspicion of murder told him he could name his fee, even offering to send him a blank cheque, if he would come to Warsaw to prove the suspect innocent. He declined, of course, but his interest in crime was keener than ever. In October 1910, he travelled to the Old Bailey to attend the trial of Dr Crippen.

May 7th

'When the carriage came out I followed it to the station. She was like one walking in her sleep, but when they tried to get her into the train she came to life and struggled. They pushed her into the carriage. She fought her way out again. I took her part, got her into a cab, and here we are. I shan't forget the face at the carriage window as I led her away. I'd have a short life if he had his way – the black-eyed, scowling, yellow devil.'

'Wisteria Lodge'

May 8th

Conan Doyle did respond to the occasional distraught letter, like the one from Joan Paynter in Hampstead: 'I am writing to you as I can think of no one else who could help me . . . About five weeks ago I met a man, a Dane. We became engaged & although I did not wish him to say anything about it for a little while he insisted on going down to Torquay to see my people . . . ' Once the wedding preparations had been made the Dane disappeared. Conan Doyle was able, by a 'process of deduction, to show her very clearly both whither he had gone and how unworthy he was of her affections'. She replied, 'I don't know how to thank you sufficiently . . . I have had an extraordinary escape . . . '

_____

_____

_____

_____

_____

_____

_____

May 9th

'Here we are, Watson – this must be the one.' He threw it open, and as he did so there was a low, harsh murmur, growing steadily into a loud roar as a train dashed past us in the darkness. Holmes swept his light along the window-sill. It was thickly coated with soot from the passing engines, but the black surface was blurred and rubbed in places.

'You can see where they rested the body. Halloa, Watson! what is this? There can be no doubt that it is a blood mark.' He was pointing to faint discolorations along the woodwork of the window. 'Here it is on the stone of the stair also. The demonstration is complete.'

'The Bruce-Partington Plans'

May 10th

Winston Churchill liked Conan Doyle's great historical novels 'even more than the detective stories'. Not only did the writer excel in both genres, but he rivalled Jules Verne and H. G. Wells in the realm of science fiction. It is likely that clues of all kinds are to be found throughout his work. Following the publication in 1912 of *The Lost World*, featuring another of his immortal characters, Professor Challenger, 'a caveman in a lounge suit', an American academic claimed that it contained several encrypted clues relating to the Piltdown Man hoax that fooled the scientific world for forty years.

May 11th

A sound of quick steps broke the silence of the moor. Crouching among the stones we stared intently at the silver-tipped bank in front of us. The steps grew louder, and through the fog, as through a curtain, there stepped the man whom we were awaiting. He looked round him in surprise as he emerged into the clear, starlit night.

The Hound of the Baskervilles

_____

_____

May 12th

In the press on 1 April 1913 was the following item: 'Sir Arthur Conan Doyle's stirring romance *The Lost World* has aroused the adventurous spirit of a party of Americans. A few days ago the yacht *Delaware* left Philadelphia and sailed away for the broad waters of the Amazon. The yacht is the property of the University of Pennsylvania and is bound for Brazil with a daring party of explorers who propose penetrating into the far reaches of the Amazon and to the headwaters of many of its tributaries in the interest of science and humanity. They seek Conan Doyle's "lost world", or some scientific evidence of it.' It seems it wasn't only Sherlock Holmes his readers believed to be real!

May 13th

'Leonardo could have saved me. If he had rushed forward and struck the beast with his club he might have cowed it. But the man lost his nerve. I heard him shout in his terror, and then I saw him turn and fly. At the same instant the teeth of the lion met in my face. Its hot, filthy breath had already poisoned me and I was hardly conscious of pain. With the palms of my hands I tried to push the great, steaming, blood-stained jaws away from me, and I screamed for help.'

'The Veiled Lodger'

May 14th

'That Sherlock Holmes was anything but mythical to many is shown by the fact that I have had many letters addressed to him with requests that I forward them. Watson has also had a number of letters in which he has been asked for the address or for the autograph of his more brilliant confrère. A press-cutting agency wrote to Watson asking whether Holmes would not wish to subscribe. When Holmes retired, several elderly ladies were ready to keep house for him and one sought to ingratiate herself by assuring me that she knew all about bee-keeping and could "segregate the queen" . . . I have often been asked whether I had myself the qualities which I depicted, or whether I was merely the Watson that I look. Of course I am well aware that it is one thing to grapple with a practical problem and quite another thing when you are allowed to solve it under your own conditions. At the same time a man cannot spin a character out of his own inner consciousness and make it really lifelike unless he has some possibilities of that character within him.'

Memories and Adventures

May 15th

Near the foot of the bed stood a dish of oranges and a carafe of water. As we passed it Holmes, to my unutterable astonishment, leaned over in front of me and deliberately knocked the whole thing over. The glass smashed into a thousand pieces and the fruit rolled about into every corner of the room.

'You've done it now, Watson,' said he, coolly. 'A pretty mess you've made of the carpet.'

'The Reigate Squires'

May 16th

Sir Sidney Roberts (1887–1966), author, publisher, biographer and noted Sherlockian, concluded from textual evidence that Sherlock Holmes was 'born in 1854 of an English father and a mother descended from a line of French painters. He seems to have been something of an aesthete at university, probably Oxford but certainly not Cambridge. On coming down from university he took rooms near the British Museum to study those sciences relevant to his intended career. In 1881, in a laboratory at St Bartholomew's Hospital, he met Dr Watson, and they decided to share the rooms in Baker Street. We know that Holmes refused a knighthood, but he did accept the Légion d'honneur. He retired to Sussex and kept bees, but of his life after 1914 there exists no record.'

_____

_____

_____

_____

_____

_____

_____

May 17th

Then he sat gazing for a moment in silent amazement at a small blue book which lay before him. Across the cover was printed in golden letters *Practical Handbook of Bee Culture*. Only for one instant did the master spy glare at this strangely irrelevant inscription. The next he was gripped at the back of his neck by a grasp of iron, and a chloroformed sponge was held in front of his writhing face.

'His Last Bow'

May 18th

Five more of the Sherlock Holmes stories which were to make up *His Last Bow* were written as the Great War loomed. Conan Doyle urged Britain to prepare for war with Germany, warning of the U-boat threat and recommending measures such as a Channel Tunnel. His efforts won him the support of the young Winston Churchill. When war broke out he wrote a pamphlet, 'To Arms', urging volunteers to enlist, and set up his own platoon. Between the winter of 1913 and the spring of 1914 he wrote his fourth and final Sherlock Holmes novel, *The Valley of Fear*. It appeared in *The Strand Magazine* from September 1914 to May 1915.

_____

_____

_____

_____

_____

_____

_____

_____

_____

May 19th

The prisoner had raised himself with some difficulty upon the sofa and was staring with a strange mixture of amazement and hatred at his captor.

'I shall get level with you . . . If it takes me all my life I shall get level with you!'

'The old sweet song,' said Holmes. 'How often have I heard it in days gone by. It was a favourite ditty of the late lamented Professor Moriarty. Colonel Sebastian Moran has also been known to warble it. And yet I live and keep bees upon the South Downs.'

'His Last Bow'

———————————————————————

———————————————————
———————————————————
———————————————————
———————————————————
———————————————————
———————————————————
———————————————————
———————————————————

May 20th

In February 1914, Greenhough Smith asked for a report on the work in progress. '*The Strand* are paying so high a price for this story that I should be churlish indeed if I refused any possible information,' was Conan Doyle's response. 'The name, I think, will be *The Valley of Fear*... As in *A Study in Scarlet* the plot goes to America for at least half the book while it recounts the events which led up to the crime in England... This part will contain one surprise which I hope will be a real staggerer to the most confirmed reader. But in the long stretch we abandon Holmes. That is necessary.' He added as an afterthought: 'I fancy this is my swan-song in fiction.'

_____

_____

_____

_____

_____

_____

_____

_____

May 21st

Just as she reached the bottom of the stairs, Mr Barker had rushed out of the study. He had stopped Mrs Douglas and begged her to go back.

'For God's sake, go back to your room!' he cried. 'Poor Jack is dead! You can do nothing. For God's sake, go back!'

The Valley of Fear

May 22nd

'His Last Bow', an 'Epilogue' about Holmes's war service and the last story of the penultimate collection of Sherlock Holmes stories, appeared in *Collier's* magazine on 22 September 1917, one month before publication of the collection, *His Last Bow: Some Reminiscences of Sherlock Holmes*. The American edition added *Later* to the subtitle. The great detective has at last laid aside his magnifying glass and retired into private life. Indeed, as Dr Watson subsequently observes, 'since he has definitely retired from London and betaken himself to study and bee-farming on the Sussex Downs, notoriety has become hateful to him.'

_____

_____

_____

_____

_____

_____

_____

_____

May 23rd

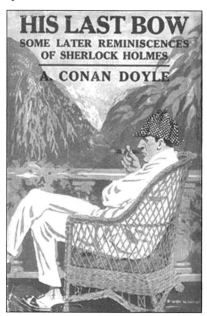

May 24th

His distinguished biographer John Dickson Carr considered that when he wrote *The Valley of Fear* and 'His Last Bow' Conan Doyle was at the 'very peak of his inventive powers'. In the last paragraph of 'His Last Bow' he has Holmes taking a positive view of the war-torn world. 'Good old Watson! You are the one fixed point in a changing age. There's an east wind coming all the same, such a wind as never blew on England yet. It will be cold and bitter, Watson, and a good many of us may wither before its blast. But it's God's own wind none the less, and a cleaner, better, stronger land will lie in the sunshine when the storm has cleared. Start her up, Watson, for it's time that we were on our way.'

May 25th

The young stranger's bold grey eyes looked back fearlessly through their glasses at the deadly black ones which turned sharply upon him.

'Well, young man, I can't call your face to mind.'

'I'm new here, Mr McGinty.'

'You are not so new that you can't give a gentleman his proper title.'

The Valley of Fear

_____

_____

_____

157

May 26th

Dr Watson added an explanatory Preface to *His Last Bow*: 'The friends of Mr Sherlock Holmes will be glad to learn that he is still alive and well, though somewhat crippled by occasional attacks of rheumatism. He has, for many years, lived in a small house upon the Downs five miles from Eastbourne, where his time is divided between philosophy and agriculture. During this period of rest he has refused the most princely offers to take up various cases, having determined that his retirement was to be a permanent one. The approach of the German war caused him, however, to lay his remarkable combination of intellectual and practical activity at the disposal of the Government, with historical results . . . Several previous experiences which have lain long in my portfolio have been added to "His Last Bow" so as to complete the volume.'

_____

_____

_____

_____

_____

_____

_____

May 27th

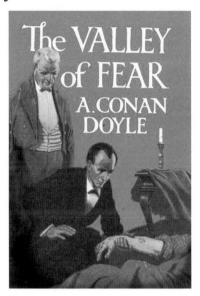

May 28th

There were more Holmes stories to come during the 1920s, but, like *The Hound of the Baskervilles*, they were written, as it were, in retrospective mode. They appeared in *The Strand* between 1921 and 1927, before being collected in *The Case Book of Sherlock Holmes*. After the tragically early death of Sidney Paget in 1908, *The Strand Magazine* was hard put to it to find an artist as inspired as he had been. For the stories between 1908 and 1917, later collected in *His Last Bow*, they used seven different illustrators; for *The Valley of Fear*, they chose Frank Wiles; and work on *The Case Book* was shared between Wiles and Howard K. Elcock.

_____

_____

_____

_____

_____

_____

_____

_____

May 29th

' "Let me say once for all that I am aware of three passages in my fiancé's life in which he became entangled with designing women, and that I am assured of his hearty repentance for any evil that he may have done."

' "Three passages!" screamed my companion. "You fool! You unutterable fool!"

' "Mr Holmes, I beg that you will bring this interview to an end," said the icy voice. "I have obeyed my father's wish in seeing you, but I am not compelled to listen to the ravings of this person." '

'The Illustrious Client'

May 30th

Roger Casement was a highly courageous man who had impressed Conan Doyle with his exposure of imperialist atrocities in the Belgian Congo. He was knighted for his investigations of human-rights abuses in Peru and his report on the Congo. A fervent Irish nationalist, he supported Germany at the outset of World War I, hoping to gain German collaboration in an Irish bid for independence. As a result he was stripped of his knighthood and, in 1916, condemned to be hanged as a traitor. Conan Doyle campaigned to save him, but in vain.

May 31st

With a joyous cry the spaniel dashed forward to the carriage and sprang upon the step. Then in a moment its eager greeting changed to furious rage, and it snapped at the black skirt above it.

'Drive on! Drive on!' shrieked a harsh voice. The coachman lashed the horses, and we were left standing in the roadway.

'Well, Watson, that's done it,' said Holmes, as he fastened the lead to the neck of the excited spaniel. 'He thought it was his mistress and he found it was a stranger. Dogs don't make mistakes.'

'Shoscombe Old Place'

JUNE

Sherlock Holmes by Arthur Ignatius Keller

June 1st

Here we had a very extraordinary interruption.

Holmes raised his hand for silence. Then he strode across the room, flung open the door, and dragged in a great gaunt woman whom he had seized by the shoulder. She entered with ungainly struggles, like some huge awkward chicken, torn squawking out of its coop. 'Leave me alone! What are you a-doin' of?' she screeched.

'The Three Gables'

June 2nd

In 1916 Conan Doyle visited British forces in France and Italy and experienced the horror of the trenches at first hand. He was intensely proud when he encountered Captain Kingsley Conan Doyle, 'my boy Kingsley, with his usual jolly grin upon his weather-stained features', who was serving in the front line. For ten nights before the Battle of the Somme, Kingsley crawled out to the German wire and marked the places where the wire was uncut to help the gunners. On the first day of the battle every officer of his battalion, the Hampshires, was either killed or wounded. Kingsley received two shrapnel bullets in the neck and was going to be out of action for a while . . .

_____

_____

_____

_____

_____

_____

_____

_____

June 3rd

'We wish a statement, Mr Scott Eccles, as to the events which led up to the death last night of Mr Aloysius Garcia, of Wisteria Lodge, near Esher.'

Our client had sat up with staring eyes and every tinge of colour struck from his astonished face.

'Dead? Did you say he was dead?'

'Yes, sir, he is dead.'

'But how? An accident?'

'Murder, if ever there was one upon earth.'

'Wisteria Lodge'

June 4th

On 28 October 1918, a fortnight before Armistice Day, Kingsley Doyle, still not wholly recovered from his wounds, succumbed to a bout of Spanish flu, the devastating influenza virus which swept the world between 1918 and 1920. The news of his death reached his father when he was on the point of addressing a meeting in Nottingham on the subject of Spiritualism. Showing no sign except 'a slight moistening of the eyes', Conan Doyle went out and gave his lecture, saying Kingsley would have wished it.

_____

_____

_____

_____

_____

_____

_____

_____

_____

June 5th

The plump young man led us to a spot where the top of one of the wooden rails had been cracked. A small fragment of the wood was hanging down. Holmes pulled it off and examined it critically.

'Do you think that was done last night? It looks rather old, does it not?'

'Well, possibly so.'

'There are no marks of anyone jumping down upon the other side. No, I fancy we shall get no help here. Let us go back to the bedroom and talk the matter over.'

'The Naval Treaty'

June 6th

During the precarious early days of his medical practice in Southsea, Conan Doyle had been greatly cheered by the company of his ten-year-old brother Innes, who joined him as his 'little knicker-bockered comrade'. It was in Southsea that Innes finished his schooling before going into the army. 'Little did I foresee that he would win distinction in the greatest of all wars and die in the prime of his manhood – but not before he knew that complete victory had been attained.' Brigadier-General John Francis Innes Hay Doyle DSO, a hero of the trenches who somehow managed to survive, died in February 1919 in the same influenza epidemic that had claimed the life of Kingsley.

June 7th

'Stop! Where are you going?'

'To Scotland Yard.'

We had not got halfway to the door before she had overtaken us and was holding his arm. She had turned in a moment from steel to velvet.

'Come and sit down, gentlemen. Let us talk this matter over. I feel that I may be frank with you, Mr Holmes. You have the feelings of a gentleman. How quick a woman's instinct is to find it out. I will treat you as a friend.'

'The Three Gables'

_____

_____

June 8th

In September 1893, Connie, one of Conan Doyle's younger sisters, married Edward 'Willie' Hornung. 'He was a Dr Johnson without the learning but with a finer wit. No one could say a neater thing, and his writings, good as they are, never adequately represented the powers of the man, nor the quickness of his brain. These things depend upon the time and the fashion, and go flat in the telling, but I remember how, when I showed him the record of someone who claimed to have done a hundred yards under ten seconds, he said: "It is a sprinter's error." Golf he could not abide, for he said it was "unsportsmanlike to hit a sitting ball". His criticism upon my Sherlock Holmes was: "Though he might be more humble, there is no police like Holmes." I think I may claim that his famous character Raffles was a kind of inversion of Sherlock Holmes, Bunny playing Watson. He admits as much in his kindly dedication.'

_____

_____

_____

_____

_____

_____

June 9th

'If you are clever enough to bring destruction upon me, rest assured that I shall do as much to you.'

'You have paid me several compliments, Mr Moriarty,' said I. 'Let me pay you one in return when I say that if I were assured of the former eventuality I would, in the interests of the public, cheerfully accept the latter.'

'I can promise you the one, but not the other,' he snarled, and so turned his rounded back upon me, and went peering and blinking out of the room.

'The Final Problem'

_____

_____

_____

_____

_____

_____

_____

June 10th

Edward Hornung and Conan Doyle were friends, although the relationship was strained by Hornung's disapproval of Conan Doyle's relationship with Jean Leckie while his first wife Louise was still alive. Hornung became most famous for his books about A. J. Raffles, the 'gentleman thief', and his sidekick, Bunny Manders, a duo modelled partly on Holmes and Watson and partly on Oscar Wilde and Lord Alfred Douglas. He and Connie had one son, Arthur Oscar, who was killed at the Second Battle of Ypres in July 1915. Hornung himself died of influenza in France in 1921.

_____

_____

_____

_____

_____

_____

_____

_____

June 11th

He took out the two ears as he spoke, and laying a
board across his knee he examined them minutely,
while Lestrade and I, bending forward on each side
of him, glanced alternately at these dreadful relics
and at the thoughtful, eager face of our companion.
Finally he returned them to the box once more and
sat for a while in deep meditation.

'You have observed, of course,' said he at last, 'that
the ears are not a pair.' . . .

'The Cardboard Box'

June 12th

Mary Doyle (neé Foley) possessed a formidable personality and was a strong influence on the lives of her children, especially that of her older son Arthur, who always referred to her affectionately as 'the Ma'am'. She instilled in him at an early age a love of the chivalric romances and a firm belief in the English code of honour. He remembered her gift for story-telling, and how her voice would sink 'to a horror-stricken whisper when she came to a crisis in her narrative'. He claimed it was to her he owed his passion for literature.

_____

_____

_____

_____

_____

_____

_____

_____

_____

June 13th

Sherlock Holmes had been bending for a long time over a low-power microscope. Now he straightened himself up and looked round at me in triumph.

'It is glue, Watson,' said he. 'Unquestionably it is glue. Have a look at these scattered objects in the field! . . . Those hairs are threads from a tweed coat. The irregular grey masses are dust. There are epithelial scales on the left. Those brown blobs in the centre are undoubtedly glue.'

'Well,' I said, laughing, 'I am prepared to take your word for it. Does anything depend upon it?'

'Shoscombe Old Place'

June 14th

With 'her sweet face, her sensitive mouth, her peering, short-sighted eyes, her general suggestion of a plump little hen who is still on the alert about her chickens', Conan Doyle's mother paid close attention to the progress of her son's career and was a valued confidante to whom he wrote countless letters over the years seeking support and advice about his writing and about his personal life. After her death in 1921, Conan Doyle devoted his time increasingly to Spiritualism.

_____

_____

_____

_____

_____

_____

_____

_____

_____

June 15th

I moved my head to look at the cabinet behind me. When I turned again Sherlock Holmes was standing smiling at me across my study table. I rose to my feet, stared at him for some seconds in utter amazement, and then it appears that I must have fainted for the first and the last time in my life . . .

'Holmes!' I cried. 'Is it really you? Can it indeed be that you are alive? Is it possible that you succeeded in climbing out of that awful abyss?'

'Wait a moment,' said he. 'Are you sure that you are really fit to discuss things? I have given you a serious shock by my unnecessarily dramatic reappearance.'

'The Empty House'

June 16th

For Conan Doyle the years leading up to his mother's death had been a catalogue of loss. 'Our household suffered terribly in the war. The first to fall was my wife's brother, Malcolm Leckie . . . Then two brave nephews, Alec Forbes and Oscar Hornung, went down with bullets through the brain. My gallant brother-in-law, Major Oldham, was killed by a sniper . . . And then, just as all seemed over, a double blow . . . my Kingsley, one of the grandest boys that ever a father was blessed with . . . it was pneumonia that slew him . . . and the same cursed plague carried off my soldier brother Innes . . . '

_____

_____

_____

_____

_____

_____

_____

June 17th

He hurried to his chamber and was down again in a few minutes dressed as a common loafer. With his collar turned up, his shiny, seedy coat, his red cravat and his worn boots, he was a perfect sample of the class.

'I think that this should do,' said he, glancing into the glass above the fireplace. 'I only wish that you could come with me, Watson, but I fear that it won't do.'

'The Beryl Coronet'

June 18th

Jean Doyle's closest friend, Lily Loder-Symonds, a gentle, fair-haired woman with a sensitive temperament, who was living at Windlesham during the war years, had three brothers killed at the Ypres Salient. A fourth brother had been wounded and taken prisoner. When Lily herself died after a short illness the Doyles were devastated. They knew that for some time before her death Lily had been developing the power of 'automatic writing' and receiving messages from the dead soldiers, 'full of military details which the girl could not know'. Doyle was impressed but not convinced. Then he received a message himself. 'I felt at last no doubt at all.'

June 19th

The window leading out to the garden was wide open. Beside it, looking like some terrible ghost, his head girt with bloody bandages, his face drawn and white, stood Sherlock Holmes. The next instant he was through the gap, and I heard the crash of his body among the laurel bushes outside. With a howl of rage the master of the house rushed after him to the open window.

And then! It was done in an instant . . .

'The Illustrious Client'

June 20th

'Automatic writing,' cautioned Conan Doyle, 'should always be regarded with suspicion, for it is easy to deceive oneself.' However, the message he had received from Malcolm Leckie was a reminiscence so intensely personal that it could have been known to no one in the world other than to Malcolm Leckie and himself. In it he found the objective proof that he had been in search of for thirty years. 'I seemed suddenly to see that this subject with which I had so long dallied [could be] a call of hope and guidance to the human race at the time of its deepest affliction.'

_____

_____

_____

_____

_____

_____

_____

_____

_____

June 21st

I lit my pipe and leaned back in my chair.

'Perhaps you will explain what you are talking about.'

My client grinned mischievously.

'I had got into the way of supposing that you knew everything without being told,' said he. 'But I will give you the facts, and I hope to God that you will be able to tell me what they mean. I've been awake all night puzzling my brain, and the more I think the more incredible does it become.'

'The Blanched Soldier'

June 22nd

'It was in the years after my marriage and before leaving Southsea that I planted the first seeds of those psychic studies which were destined to revolutionise my views and to absorb finally all the energies of my life.' Conan Doyle's article in the magazine *Light* on 21 October 1916 announced his belief in communication with the dead. 'It is absolute lunacy, or it is a revolution in religious thought; a revolution that gives us an immense consolation when those who are dear to us pass behind the veil.'

June 23rd

Holmes smiled and clapped Lestrade upon the shoulder.

'Instead of being ruined, my good sir, you will find that your reputation has been enormously enhanced. Just make a few alterations in that report which you were writing, and they will understand how hard it is to throw dust in the eyes of Inspector Lestrade.'

'And you don't want your name to appear?'

'Not at all . . . '

'The Norwood Builder'

June 24th

Parapsychologist Sir William Barrett, courtesy of the editor of *Light*, thanked Conan Doyle for his 'brave and timely article . . . Nearly a quarter of a century ago, Sir Arthur – then Dr – Conan Doyle took the chair at a lecture on psychical research delivered by me at the Upper Norwood Literary Society, of which he was president . . . Dr Conan Doyle, in moving a vote of thanks, referred to the deep interest he had maintained for many years in the subject of the lecture, and also to some past experiences of his own.'

_____

_____

_____

_____

_____

_____

_____

_____

_____

June 25th

Holmes held up the paper so that the sunlight shone full upon it. It was a page torn from a notebook. The markings were done in pencil, and ran in this way:

Holmes examined it for some time, and then, folding it carefully up, he placed it in his pocketbook.

'The Dancing Man'

June 26th

Hitherto unconvinced, Lady Conan Doyle now shared his belief and supported her husband when he declared, 'I must proclaim it.' Over the previous forty years he had written not only a number of major best-sellers, from *The White Company* to *The Lost World*, and chronicled the activities of his three heroes, Sherlock Holmes, Professor Challenger and Brigadier Gerard (a flamboyant adventurer of the Napoleonic Wars), but he had also become an accomplished and versatile lecturer. Now, in addition to his war lectures, he offered lectures on Spiritualism to his eager public. And all this at a time when he was engaged upon his *History of the British Campaign in France and Flanders*, in six volumes (1916–1920).

June 27th

'Fancy anyone having the heart to hurt him,' he muttered, as he glanced down at the small, angry red pucker upon the cherub throat.

It was at this moment that I chanced to glance at Holmes, and saw a most singular intentness in his expression. His face was as set as if it had been carved out of old ivory, and his eyes, which had glanced for a moment at father and child, were now fixed with eager curiosity upon something at the other side of the room. Following his gaze I could only guess that he was looking out through the window at the melancholy, dripping garden.

'The Sussex Vampire'

June 28th

In 1924, Conan Doyle at last succeeded in mounting an exhibition of his father's work in the West End, the fulfilment of a long-held ambition. He also bought a handsome thatched house, Bignell Wood, in the romantic setting of the New Forest. Here he completed his controversial two-volume *History of Spiritualism*; at the same time the impatiently awaited *Case Book of Sherlock Holmes* appeared on the bookstalls. Ironically, he who could command ten shillings a word if he would write about Holmes must now pay for publication of his books if he insisted upon writing on psychical matters.

June 29th

He sank with a deep groan on to the settee and buried his face in his manacled hands . . .

'I have nothing to hide from you, gentlemen,' said he. 'If I shot the man he had his shot at me, and there's no murder in that. But if you think I could have hurt that woman, then you don't know either me or her. I tell you there was never a man in this world loved a woman more than I loved her. I had a right to her. She was pledged to me years ago. Who was this Englishman that he should come between us? I tell you that I had the first right to her, and that I was only claiming my own.'

'The Dancing Men'

June 30th

When the question of a peerage arose, Conan Doyle's second cousin, the Right Reverend Monsignor Richard Barry-Doyle, went down to Windlesham for talks. Conan Doyle may have been a personal friend of King George V, but he had enemies in high places. In England, the country of religious liberty, a peer of the realm could not be a Spiritualist.

_____

_____

_____

_____

_____

_____

_____

_____

_____

_____

_____

_____

JULY

THE COMING
OF THE FAIRIES

ARTHUR CONAN DOYLE

July 1st

Convinced of physical existence after death, Conan Doyle believed that the soul was 'a complete duplicate of the body'. When news came from Yorkshire of a series of five photographs of what appeared to be fairies, taken by two young cousins, Elsie Wright who was sixteen and Frances Griffiths who was nine, in Cottingly, he had no doubt they really were fairies. He used the photographs to illustrate an article he had been commissioned to write for the Christmas edition of *The Strand* in 1920, interpreting them as clear and visible psychic phenomena. The reading public were rather more sceptical.

July 2nd

Holmes traced his way to the farther side of a great beech and lay down once more upon his face with a little cry of satisfaction. For a long time he remained there, turning over the leaves and dried sticks, gathering up what seemed to me to be dust into an envelope and examining with his lens not only the ground but even the bark of the tree as far as he could reach.

'The Boscombe Valley Mystery'

_____

_____

_____

_____

_____

_____

July 3rd

Press coverage of the Cottingly Fairies was a mixture of 'embarrassment and puzzlement'. Maurice Hewlett, in *John O' London's Weekly*, concluded: 'Knowing children, and knowing that Sir Arthur Conan Doyle has legs, I decide that the girls have pulled one of them.' The *Truth*, in Sydney, agreed: 'What is wanted is not a knowledge of occult phenomena but a knowledge of children.' More sympathetic was the educational and social reformer Margaret McMillan: 'How wonderful that to these dear children such a wonderful gift has been vouchsafed.'

_____

_____

_____

_____

_____

_____

_____

_____

_____

July 4th

Finding that Holmes was too absorbed for conversation I had tossed aside the barren paper, and leaning back in my chair I fell into a brown study. Suddenly my companion's voice broke in upon my thoughts.

'You are right, Watson,' said he. 'It does seem a most preposterous way of settling a dispute.'

'Most preposterous!' I exclaimed, and then suddenly realising how he had echoed the inmost thought of my soul, I sat up in my chair and stared at him in blank amazement.

'The Cardboard Box'

_____

_____

_____

_____

_____

July 5th

In 1966, a reporter from the *Daily Express* traced Elsie and Frances and they admitted that they had faked four of the photographs using cardboard cut-outs made from pictures in their copy of *Princess Mary's Gift Book*; but the fifth, Frances insisted, was genuine. At the time, Conan Doyle was convinced by them all and stated so openly in *The Coming of the Fairies*. The ridicule that this occasioned was a matter of indifference to him. In 1985, the old ladies said they had been too embarrassed to admit to having taken in the creator of Sherlock Holmes.

July 6th

'Yes,' said our ally, 'I *am* Bob Carruthers, and I'll see this woman righted if I have to swing for it. I told you what I'd do if you molested her, and, by the Lord, I'll be as good as my word!'

'You're too late. She's my wife!'

'No, she's your widow.'

His revolver cracked, and I saw the blood spurt from the front of Woodley's waistcoat.

'The Solitary Cyclist'

July 7th

Throughout the stories, Sherlock Holmes denies any belief in the supernatural. Conan Doyle explained that he had set Holmes up as a calculating machine who must, as a result, click with absolute consistency from beginning to end. Conan Doyle was often to be found in the Psychic Bookshop in London's Victoria Street, a vital resource for the Spiritualist community which he established in 1925. It was presided over by his daughter Mary, herself a believer. 'Why do you go on hammering at proof and proof and proof? We know these things are true. Why do you try to prove it by so many examples?' 'You have never been a rationalist,' was her father's reply.

_____

_____

_____

_____

_____

_____

_____

_____

July 8th

'Get down, Watson!' cried Holmes, with a heavy hand upon my shoulder. We had hardly sunk from view when the man flew past us on the road. Amid a rolling cloud of dust I caught a glimpse of a pale, agitated face – a face with horror in every lineament, the mouth open, the eyes staring wildly in front.

'The Priory School'

July 9th

Conan Doyle was always ready for debate on the subject of Spiritualism. In 1920 he was challenged at Queen's Hall in London by the well-known sceptic Joseph McCabe, who tried to convince him he was being duped. A famous psychical researcher Harry Price was attacked by Conan Doyle for exposing the spirit photographer William Hope as a fraud, although Price was absolutely right. Conan Doyle was repeatedly taken in by clever 'psychics' up to all sorts of trickery who were later discredited and who would have been seen through at once by his alter ego Sherlock Holmes. It was all very paradoxical. Conan Doyle spoke in a filmed interview about Sherlock Holmes and Spiritualism recorded in 1927.

July 10th

He had had one of those violent strains of the ankle which leave a man helpless. With difficulty he limped up to the door, where a squat, dark, elderly man was smoking a black clay pipe.

'How are you, Mr Reuben Hayes?' said Holmes.

'Who are you, and how do you get my name so pat?' the countryman answered, with a suspicious flash of a pair of cunning eyes.

'Well, it's printed on the board above your head.'

'The Priory School'

July 11th

Harry Houdini, the celebrated American magician and escapologist, became a fierce opponent of Spiritualism following his experience of fraudulent mediums (of whom one was Lady Conan Doyle) after the death of his beloved mother. He and Conan Doyle were friends but the friendship could not last. Conan Doyle was sure that Houdini had supernatural powers and Houdini was unable to convince him that his feats were merely illusions. On one occasion Houdini performed an impressive trick specifically to demonstrate to Conan Doyle the foolishness of endorsing phenomena simply because there seemed to be no explanation. Inevitably, the two had an acrimonious falling-out.

July 12th

Mr Sherlock Holmes was leaning back in his chair after his whimsical protest, and was unfolding his morning paper in a leisurely fashion, when our attention was arrested by a tremendous ring at the bell, followed immediately by a hollow drumming sound, as if someone were beating on the outer door with his fist. As it opened there came a tumultuous rush into the hall, rapid feet clattered up the stair, and an instant later a wild-eyed and frantic young man, pale, dishevelled and palpitating, burst into the room.

'The Norwood Builder'

July 13th

Delivering lectures, writing articles, promoting his books and travelling tirelessly to most corners of the world (usually with his family in tow), Conan Doyle spent at least £250,000 spreading the 'truth' about Spiritualism. In November of 1929 he made a point of returning to London for the Armistice Memorial Service. His latest lecture tour, of Holland and Scandinavia, had exhausted him, but he was determined to speak as arranged at the Albert Hall and the Queen's Hall. He even addressed the crowds from a balcony, bare-headed and in the falling snow. But he was suffering from angina pectoris and his heart was under great strain.

_____

_____

_____

_____

_____

_____

_____

_____

_____

July 14th

Holmes had been examining the cover of the note-book with his magnifying lens.

'Surely there is some discoloration here,' said he.

'Yes, sir, it is a bloodstain. I told you that I picked the book off the floor.'

'Was the bloodstain above or below?'

'On the side next the boards.'

'Which proves, of course, that the book was dropped after the crime was committed.'

'Exactly, Mr Holmes. I appreciated that point, and I conjectured that it was dropped by the murderer in his hurried flight. It lay near the door.'

'Black Peter'

July 15th

Back at Windlesham, surrounded by the people and things he loved, he survived through the spring of 1930, but his legendary strength was failing. Early on the morning of 7 July, his family helped him from his bed into his familiar basket chair from where he could look out over the garden, always specially beautiful in the summer months. And it was there he died, peacefully, murmuring to his wife Jean how wonderful she was. At his death, the world went into mourning.

_____

_____

_____

_____

_____

_____

_____

_____

_____

July 16th

The nocturnal visitor was a young man, frail and thin, with a black moustache which intensified the deadly pallor of his face . . . I have never seen any human being who appeared to be in such a pitiable fright, for his teeth were visibly chattering and he was shaking in every limb . . . We watched him staring round with frightened eyes. Then he laid the candle-end upon the table and disappeared from our view into one of the corners. He returned with a large book, one of the logbooks which formed a line upon the shelves. Leaning on the table he rapidly turned over the leaves of this volume until he came to the entry which he sought.

'Black Peter'

July 17th

The *New York Times* announced: 'Sir Arthur Conan Doyle, creator of Sherlock Holmes and noted Spiritualist, died today at his home in Crowborough, Sussex. He was seventy-one years old. Sir Arthur claimed to have had conversations with the spirits of Cecil Rhodes, Earl Haig, Joseph Conrad and others. Adrian Conan Doyle said the whole family believed he would continue to keep in touch with them . . . '
In his later years Sir Arthur often expressed a wish to be remembered for his psychic work . . . He confessed he was tired of hearing about his celebrated character Sherlock Holmes. 'Holmes is dead,' he said. 'I have done with him.'

_____

_____

_____

_____

_____

_____

_____

_____

July 18th

Holmes had in some way ruffled our visitor, whose chubby face had assumed a far less amiable expression.

'Patience! Patience, Mr Garrideb!' said my friend in a soothing voice. 'Dr Watson would tell you that these little digressions of mine sometimes prove in the end to have some bearing on the matter. But why did Mr Nathan Garrideb not come with you?'

'The Three Garridebs'

July 19th

Any controversy concerning his burial place, since he was avowedly not a Christian but a Spiritualist, was forestalled when it was decided to bury him beside the summer-house in the garden at Windlesham. At the funeral on 11 July his family and members of the Spiritualist community celebrated rather than mourned his 'passing behind the veil'. The grave was marked with a simple oak slab bearing the words: 'Steel True, Blade Straight'. On 13 July, thousands filled the Albert Hall for a séance during which Estelle Roberts, a Spiritualist medium, claimed to have contacted Sir Arthur.

_____

_____

_____

_____

_____

_____

_____

_____

July 20th

'I think the fellow is really an American, but he has worn his accent smooth with years of London. What is his game, then, and what motive lies behind this preposterous search for Garridebs? It's worth our attention, for, granting that the man is a rascal, he is certainly a complex and ingenious one. We must now find out if our other correspondent is a fraud also. Just ring him up, Watson.'

I did so, and heard a thin, quavering voice at the other end of the line.

My friend took the instrument . . .

'The Three Garridebs'

_____

_____

_____

_____

_____

_____

_____

_____

July 21st

It was when Conan Doyle was researching *The White Company* that he discovered the beauty of the New Forest and as a result bought a house near Minstead as a birthday present for his wife Jean. The postman refused to deliver mail to Bignell Wood because it was there that the couple were said to hold séances. It was rumoured that Charles Dickens and Joseph Conrad had come through to ask Conan Doyle to complete their unfinished work. Jean died in 1940 and was buried with her husband at Windlesham, but when that house was sold 1955 their remains were reinterred under a tree in Minstead's ancient churchyard.

July 22nd

Clearly our moment had come. Holmes touched my wrist as a signal, and together we stole across to the open trapdoor. Gently as we moved, however, the old floor must have creaked under our feet, for the head of our American, peering anxiously round, emerged suddenly from the open space. His face turned upon us with a glare of baffled rage, which gradually softened into a rather shamefaced grin as he realised that two pistols were pointed at his head.

'The Three Garridebs'

July 23rd

Undershaw, the house Conan Doyle had built at Hindhead, was the family home from 1891 to 1907. Some years after they left, the house became a hotel and remained so until 2004 when it was sold to a developer. Conservationists and Conan Doyle enthusiasts have fought to preserve it, however, and the house has stood empty while the battle rages. In 2012, the High Court ruled that redevelopment permission be quashed because proper procedure had not been followed. The future of the house is still in the balance.

July 24th

Holmes pointed to the street lamp above our heads.

'He could see what he was doing here and he could not there. That was his reason.'

'By Jove! that's true,' said the detective. 'Now that I come to think of it, Dr Barnicot's bust was broken not far from his red lamp. Well, Mr Holmes, what are we to do with that fact?'

'The Six Napoleons'

_____

_____

_____

_____

_____

_____

_____

_____

_____

_____

July 25th

The inscription on Conan Doyle's gravestone reads:

STEEL TRUE
BLADE STRAIGHT
ARTHUR CONAN DOYLE
KNIGHT
PATRIOT, PHYSICIAN,
& MAN OF LETTERS
22 MAY 1858 – 7 JULY 1930
AND HIS BELOVED, HIS WIFE
JEAN CONAN DOYLE
REUNITED 27 JUNE 1940

There is a bronze statue of the writer by David Cornell in Crowborough, where Conan Doyle lived for twenty-three years. A splendid bronze sculpted by John Doubleday of Sherlock Holmes stands outside Baker Street tube station near his famous rooms at 221B Baker Street. There are other statues of Sherlock Holmes by Doubleday below the Reichenbach Falls in Switzerland, in Edinburgh and in Japan.

July 26th

But the production of the photograph had a remarkable effect upon the manager. His face flushed with anger, and his brows knotted over his blue Teutonic eyes. 'Ah, the rascal!' he cried. 'Yes, indeed, I know him very well. This has always been a respectable establishment, and the only time that we have ever had the police in it was over this very fellow. It was more than a year ago now. He knifed another Italian in the street . . . '

'The Six Napoleons'

July 27th

In his will, Conan Doyle left all the royalties from his huge number of highly successful books, which amounted to many millions of pounds over the following decades, to his second wife and their three children. To Mary, his daughter by his first wife Louise, who was born in Southsea in 1889, he left just two thousand pounds. Mary had been a devoted daughter and had always supported her father in his Spiritualist crusade. After his death she continued to run the Psychic Bookshop he founded in London's Victoria Street and died, unmarried, in 1976.

_____

_____

_____

_____

_____

_____

_____

_____

_____

July 28th

'Well, I am an honest man, though not a very rich one. I only gave fifteen shillings for the bust, and I think you ought to know that before I take ten pounds from you.'

'I am sure the scruple does you honour, Mr Sandeford. But I have named that price, so I intend to stick to it.'

'The Six Napoleons'

July 29th

Conan Doyle's widow chose a Spiritualist, the Reverend John Lamond, to write *Arthur Conan Doyle: A Memoir* (1931), a biography that majored on Sir Arthur's interest in the paranormal. Unsurprisingly, the public wanted to read about the creator of Sherlock Holmes, so after their mother's death the two sons grudgingly allowed Hesketh Pearson to write *Conan Doyle: His Life and Art* (1943). They denounced the book, however, as a 'fakeography', and Adrian took it upon himself to write *The True Conan Doyle* (1945).

_____

_____

_____

_____

_____

_____

_____

_____

_____

July 30th

'The moment I looked at my table I was aware that someone had rummaged among my papers. The proof was in three long slips. I had left them all together. Now, I found that one of them was lying on the floor, one was on the side table near the window, and the third was where I had left it.'

Holmes stirred for the first time.

'The first page on the floor, the second in the window, the third where you left it,' said he.

'Exactly, Mr Holmes. You amaze me. How could you possibly know that?'

'The Three Students'

July 31st

After Conan Doyle's death, his two surviving sons continued to give talks promoting Spiritualism and ran the Conan Doyle estate. Denis, born in 1909, his elder son by his second wife, married Nina M'diviani, a Georgian princess, in 1930, and died in 1955. In 1970, his widow Nina bought the estate using a loan from the Royal Bank of Scotland. She established Baskerville Investments Limited on the Isle of Man, a well-known tax haven, but soon fell behind on the loan, whereupon the bank took possession of the rights to the works of Conan Doyle. The bank sold the rights to Lady Etelka Duncan, whose daughter administers the Sir Arthur Conan Doyle Literary Trust to this day.

_____

_____

_____

_____

_____

_____

_____

AUGUST

STEEL TRUE
BLADE STRAIGHT
ARTHUR CONAN DOYLE
KNIGHT
PATRIOT, PHYSICIAN,
& MAN OF LETTERS
22 MAY 1858 – 7 JULY 1930
AND HIS BELOVED, HIS WIFE
JEAN CONAN DOYLE
REUNITED 27 JUNE 1940

Headstone inscription,
Minstead churchyard, Hampshire

August 1st

Adrian Conan Doyle, born in 1910, was the younger son of the second marriage and became his father's literary executor after his mother's death in 1940. He tried to emulate his father as a literary man of action – racing driver, big-game hunter, explorer, writer – but remained a pale shadow. In the early 1950s, with the aid of John Dickson Carr, Adrian produced a collection of Sherlock Holmes stories developed from ideas his father had made reference to but had never pursued. These stories were published as *The Exploits of Sherlock Holmes* in 1954. Adrian founded the Sir Arthur Conan Doyle Foundation in 1965.

August 2nd

A tall, flaxen-haired, slim young fellow opened it, and made us welcome when he understood our errand. There were some really curious pieces of medieval domestic architecture within. Holmes was so charmed with one of them that he insisted on drawing it in his notebook, broke his pencil, had to borrow one from our host, and finally borrowed a knife to sharpen his own. The same curious accident happened to him in the rooms of the Indian . . .

'The Three Students'

_____

_____

_____

August 3rd

The little girl Houdini called a tomboy, the daughter of Conan Doyle's second marriage, grew up to be Air Commandant Dame Lena Jean Annette Conan Doyle, Lady Bromet, DBE AE WRAF ADC. Born in 1912, she was a lively child who signed her letters to her father 'Your loving son', and liked to be called Billy. On her tenth birthday, however, she announced that she had decided to be a girl after all. She went on to pursue a highly distinguished career in the Women's Auxilliary Air Force (later the WRAF), serving in Intelligence during World War II and steadily rising in rank until her retirement in 1966. She was married to Air Vice-Marshal Sir Geoffrey Rhodes Bromet.

August 4th

In an instant he had whisked out a revolver from his breast and had fired two shots. I felt a sudden hot sear as if a red-hot iron had been pressed to my thigh. There was a crash as Holmes's pistol came down on the man's head. I had a vision of him sprawling upon the floor with blood running down his face while Holmes rummaged him for weapons. Then my friend's wiry arms were round me and he was leading me to a chair.

'You're not hurt, Watson? For God's sake, say that you are not hurt?'

'The Three Garridebs'

_____

_____

_____

August 5th

Upon the death of her brother Adrian in 1970, Jean Conan Doyle became her father's literary executor and the legal copyright holder to some of the rights to the Sherlock Holmes character as well as to her father's other works. She said that Sherlock Holmes was the family curse because of the bitter fighting over copyrights. She and the widows of her brothers initially shared control of the Sir Arthur Conan Doyle Literary Trust, but the three women did not get on. Denis's widow bought the bulk of the estate later in 1970, but Jean managed to regain the US rights in 1976.

August 6th

'Did you dust this bureau yesterday morning?'

'Yes, sir.'

'Did you notice this scratch?'

'No, sir, I did not.'

'I am sure you did not, for a duster would have swept away these shreds of varnish. Who has the key of this bureau?'

'The Professor keeps it on his watch-chain.'

'Is it a simple key?'

'No, sir; it is a Chubb's key.'

'The Golden Pince-Nez'

August 7th

Dame Jean Conan Doyle died in 1984. She bequeathed what copyrights she still owned to the Royal National Institute for the Blind, an organisation in which she had long had a personal interest because her eyesight had been poor from an early age. Subsequently the RNIB sold the rights back to the Doyle heirs. There are now nine surviving Doyle heirs, of whom none are direct descendants; although Conan Doyle had five children none of them had children of their own. His fictional works, including those concerning Sherlock Holmes, his immortal offspring, passed into the public domain in the UK in 1980.

_____

_____

_____

_____

_____

_____

_____

_____

August 8th

Again the Professor burst into high-keyed laughter. He had risen to his feet and his eyes glowed like embers.

'You are mad!' he cried. 'You are talking insanely. I helped her to escape? Where is she now?'

'She is there,' said Holmes, and he pointed to a high bookcase in the corner of the room.

I saw the old man throw up his arms, a terrible convulsion passed over his grim face, and he fell back in his chair. At the same instant the bookcase at which Holmes pointed swung round upon a hinge, and a woman rushed out into the room. 'You are right!' she cried, in a strange foreign voice. 'You are right! I am here.'

'The Golden Pince-Nez'

August 9th

In May 2004, a priceless 'lost archive' of Conan Doyle's letters, papers (including a draft of *A Study in Scarlet*) and personal effects came up for auction at Christie's, causing widespread dismay and controversy. The material, which had been the property of Adrian Conan Doyle's widow, Danish-born Anna Anderson, had been gathering dust since her death. Richard Lancelyn Green, Conan Doyle scholar and expert, tried to block the auction, arguing that in its entirety the collection should go to the British Library as Dame Jean would have wished.

_____

_____

_____

_____

_____

_____

_____

_____

_____

August 10th

'These are my last words,' said she; 'here is the packet which will save Alexis . . . Take it! You will deliver it at the Russian Embassy. Now I have done my duty, and – '

'Stop her!' cried Holmes. He bounded across the room and wrenched a small phial from her hand.

'Too late!' she said, sinking back on the bed. 'Too late! I took the poison before I left my hiding-place. My head swims! I am going! I charge you, sir, to remember the packet.'

'The Golden Pince-Nez'

August 11th

Probably the world's foremost Conan Doyle scholar, Richard Lancelyn Green had been an obsessive collector of Doyleiana and Sherlockiana since he was a child. In March 2004 he was acutely distressed about the coming sale of archive material at Christie's and feared his life might be in danger because of his opposition to it. On the night of the 27th he was found face downwards on his bed garrotted with a shoelace that had been tightened by means of a wooden spoon. Some thought he had staged his suicide to look like murder and cast suspicion on a third party, thus replicating events in one of the last Holmes mysteries 'The Problem of Thor Bridge'. The coroner returned an open verdict.

August 12th

This man is the greatest financial power in the world, and a man, as I understand, of most violent and formidable character. He married a wife, the victim of this tragedy, of whom I know nothing save that she was past her prime, which was the more unfortunate as a very attractive governess superintended the education of two young children. These are the three people concerned, and the scene is a grand old manor-house, the centre of a historical English estate. Then as to the tragedy. The wife was found in the grounds nearly half a mile from the house, late at night, clad in her dinner dress, with a shawl over her shoulders and a revolver bullet through her brain.

'Thor Bridge'

_____

_____

_____

_____

_____

_____

_____

_____

August 13th

Richard Lancelyn Green bequeathed his immense collection of Doyleiana – he was only fifty when he died and it was surely already the largest ever held in private hands – to the City of Portsmouth. It took a team of ten people two weeks to fill twelve vans with approximately fourteen thousand volumes (among them first editions of all Conan Doyle's novels and stories, poems and plays) and two hundred thousand other items – even including a re-creation of Sherlock Holmes's Baker Street study. The downside of this magnificent bequest for Portsmouth Museum was the prospect of years of cataloguing.

_____

_____

_____

_____

_____

_____

_____

_____

August 14th

I turned over the paper. 'This never came by post. How did you get it?'

'I would rather not answer that question. It has really nothing to do with the matter which you are investigating. But anything which bears upon that I will most freely answer.'

She blushed and seemed confused.

'The Lion's Mane'

August 15th

In certain of the Sherlock Holmes stories reference is made to the Baker Street Irregulars, the ubiquitous street children Holmes uses as intelligence agents. Led by an older boy, Wiggins, members of this group of urchins are paid a shilling a day (plus expenses) to be his eyes and ears on the street. For a vital clue Holmes was prepared to pay a guinea. They first appeared in *A Study in Scarlet* and they also have a role in *The Sign of The Four*.

August 16th

A woman, young and beautiful, was lying dead upon the bed. Her calm, pale face, with dim, wide-opened blue eyes, looked upwards from amid a great tangle of golden hair. At the foot of the bed, half sitting, half kneeling, his face buried in the clothes, was a young man, whose frame was racked by his sobs. So absorbed was he by his bitter grief that he never looked up until Holmes's hand was on his shoulder.

'Are you Mr Godfrey Staunton?'

'Yes, yes; I am – but you are too late. She is dead.'

'The Missing Three-Quarter'

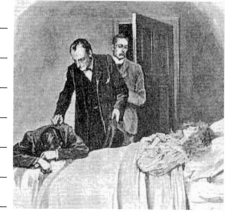

August 17th

With headquarters at 64 Baker Street, the Special Operations Executive (SOE), founded by Winston Churchill during the Second World War to 'set Europe ablaze', is sometimes referred to as the Baker Street Irregulars after Conan Doyle's fictional group. There is also a club of Sherlock Holmes enthusiasts, set up in 1934 and calling itself by that title, whose members assume names taken from the stories. In recent years the name has been adopted by a London astronomical society, the Baker Street Irregular Astronomers.

August 18th

Our guide paused at the mouth of this bridge, and he pointed to the ground.

'That was where Mrs Gibson's body lay. I marked it by that stone.'

'I understand that you were there before it was moved?'

'Yes; they sent for me at once.'

'Who did?'

'Mr Gibson himself.'

'Thor Bridge'

_____

_____

_____

_____

_____

_____

_____

_____

_____

August 19th

Of the fifty-six stories Conan Doyle wrote about Sherlock Holmes, all but four are narrated by his friend and biographer Dr John H. Watson. There are two narrated by Holmes himself ('The Adventure of the Lion's Mane' and 'The Adventure of the Blanched Soldier'), and two written in the third person ('The Adventure of the Mazarin Stone' and 'His Last Bow'). Over the years, the reading public were alert to the subtlest changes in their hero. Post Reichenbach Falls a Cornish boatman remarked to Conan Doyle: 'I think, sir, when Holmes fell over that cliff he may not have killed himself but he was never quite the same man afterwards.'

_____

_____

_____

_____

_____

_____

_____

_____

August 20th

'Meaning that I lie.'

'Well, I was trying to express it as delicately as I could, but if you insist upon the word I will not contradict you.'

I sprang to my feet, for the expression upon the millionaire's face was fiendish in its intensity, and he had raised his great knotted fist.

Holmes smiled languidly and reached his hand out for his pipe. 'Don't be noisy, Mr Gibson. I find that after breakfast even the smallest argument is unsettling. I suggest that a stroll in the morning air and a little quiet thought will be greatly to your advantage.'

'Thor Bridge'

August 21st

A perplexingly 'undiscovered' Sherlock Holmes story was reported to have been found by Adrian Conan Doyle in September 1942. In spite of family doubts, the story was published as 'The Case of the Man Who Was Wanted' on both sides of the Atlantic six years later. Hesketh Pearson's review of the story prompted an architect named Arthur Whitaker to reply: 'My pride is not unduly hurt by your remark that "The Man Who Was Wanted" is certainly not up to scratch, for the sting is much mitigated by your going on to remark that it carries the authentic trademark! This is a great compliment to my one and only effort at plagiarism.'

_____

_____

_____

_____

_____

_____

_____

_____

August 22nd

'Think once more, Lady Brackenstall. Would it not be better to be frank?'

For an instant there was hesitation in her beautiful face. Then some new strong thought caused it to set like a mask.

'I have told you all I know.'

Holmes took his hat and shrugged his shoulders. 'I am sorry,' he said, and without another word we left the room and the house. There was a pond in the park, and to this my friend led the way. It was frozen over, but a single hole was left for the convenience of a solitary swan.

'The Abbey Grange'

_____

_____

_____

_____

_____

_____

_____

_____

August 23rd

Writing in *The New Age* for 13 September 1917, Ezra Pound asserted: 'Sir A. Conan Doyle has never stooped to literature. Wells, Benett [*sic*], and the rest of them have wobbled about in penumbras, but here is the man who has "done it", who has contributed a word to the language, a character to the fiction of the Caucasian world, for there is no European language in which the Great Detective can be hid under any disguise. Herlock Sholmes, spell it as you like, is *known*. Caines and Corellis lie by the wayside. Sherlock has held us all spellbound.'

August 24th

'Well, Watson, what do you make of this?' asked Holmes, after a long pause.

'It is an amazing coincidence.'

'A coincidence! Here is one of the three men whom we had named as possible actors in this drama, and he meets a violent death during the very hours when we know that that drama was being enacted. The odds are enormous against its being coincidence. No figures could express them. No, my dear Watson, the two events are connected – *must* be connected. It is for us to find the connection.'

'The Second Stain'

August 25th

'G. K. Chesterton once remarked,' wrote Conan Doyle's biographer Hesketh Pearson, 'that if Dickens had written the Holmes stories he would have made every character as vivid as Holmes. We may reply that if Dickens had done so he would have ruined the stories, which depend for their effect on the radiance of the central character and the relative glimmer of the satellites. True, Watson's glimmer amounts to genius, but it adds to the splendour of Holmes, and Dickens would have made a fearful mess of Watson.'

_____

_____

_____

_____

_____

_____

_____

_____

_____

August 26th

The lady sprang to her feet, with the colour all dashed in an instant from her beautiful face. Her eyes glazed – she tottered – I thought that she would faint. Then with a grand effort she rallied from the shock, and a supreme astonishment and indignation chased every other expression from her features.

'You – you insult me, Mr Holmes.'

'Come, come, madam, it is useless. Give up the letter.'

She darted to the bell.

'The butler shall show you out.'

'The Second Stain'

_____

_____

_____

_____

_____

_____

_____

_____

August 27th

To a reader who suggested that the stories in the *Case Book* were not on a level with the earlier ones, Conan Doyle wrote: 'I read with interest and without offence your remarks about the Holmes stories. I could not be offended for I have never taken them seriously myself. But still, even in the humblest things there are degrees, and I wonder if the smaller impression which they produce upon you may not be due to the fact that we become blasé and stale ourselves as we grow older. My own youthful favourites no longer appeal . . . I have always said that I would utterly abolish him the moment he got below his level, but up to now, save for your note, I have seen no sign that he has lost his grip.'

August 28th

The Premier snatched the blue envelope from his hand.

'Yes, it is it – and the letter is intact. Hope, I con-gratulate you.'

'Thank you! Thank you! What a weight from my heart. But this is inconceivable – impossible. Mr Holmes, you are a wizard, a sorcerer! How did you know it was there?'

'Because I knew it was nowhere else.'

'The Second Stain'

August 29th

After the tragic sinking of the *Titanic* in April 1912, Conan Doyle and Bernard Shaw conducted a disputatious correspondence in the press on the subject. Writing to the editor of the newspaper concerned Conan Doyle closed the exchange with quiet dignity: 'Sir – Without continuing a controversy which must be sterile, I would touch on only one point . . . He says that I accused him of lying. I have been guilty of no such breach . . . The worst I think or say of Mr Shaw is that his many brilliant gifts do not include the power of weighing the evidence, nor has he that quality – call it good taste, humanity, or what you will – which prevents a man from needlessly hurting the feelings of others.'

August 30th

'There you have the whole truth of it. You can hang me, or do what you like with me, but you cannot punish me as I have been punished already. I cannot shut my eyes but I see those two faces staring at me – staring at me as they stared when my boat broke through the haze. I killed them quick, but they are killing me slow . . . '

'The Cardboard Box'

SEPTEMBER

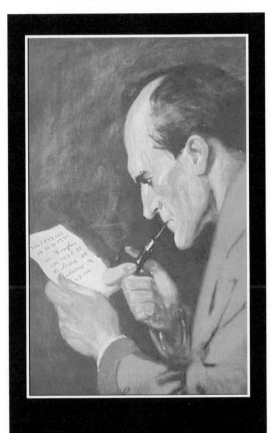

September 1st

But Mr Baynes had kept his most sinister exhibit to the last. From under the sink he drew a zinc pail which contained a quantity of blood. Then from the table he took a platter heaped with small pieces of charred bone.

'Something has been killed and something has been burned. We raked all these out of the fire. We had a doctor in this morning. He says that they are not human.'

Holmes smiled and rubbed his hands.

'Wisteria Lodge'

_____

_____

_____

_____

_____

_____

_____

259

September 2nd

'My mind rebels at stagnation. Give me problems, give me work, give me the most abstruse cryptogram, or the most intricate analysis, and I am in my own proper atmosphere. I can dispense then with artificial stimulants. But I abhor the dull routine of existence. I crave for mental exaltation. That is why I have chosen my own particular profession, or rather created it, for I am the only one in the world.'

Sherlock Holmes, *The Sign of The Four*

September 3rd

It was on a bitterly cold and frosty morning during the winter of 1897 that I was awakened by a tugging at my shoulder. It was Holmes. The candle in his hand shone upon his eager, stooping face and told me at a glance that something was amiss.

'Come, Watson, come!' he cried. 'The game is afoot. Not a word! Into your clothes and come!'

'The Abbey Grange'

261

September 4th

'In "The Adventure of the Priory School" Holmes remarks in his offhand way that by looking at a bicycle track on a damp moor one can say which way it was heading. I had so many remonstrances upon this point, varying from pity to anger, that I took out my bicycle and tried. I had imagined that the observations of the way in which the track of the hind wheel over-laid the track of the front one when the machine was not running dead straight would show the direction. I found that my correspondents were right and I was wrong, for this would be the same whichever way the cycle was moving. On the other hand the real solution was much simpler, for on an undulating moor the wheels make a much deeper impression uphill and a more shallow one downhill, so Holmes was justified of his wisdom after all.'

Memories and Adventures

September 5th

'Come, Watson, we must really take a risk and try to investigate this a little more closely.'

Together we stole down to the road and crept across to the door of the inn. The bicycle still leaned against the wall. Holmes struck a match and held it to the back wheel, and I heard him chuckle as the light fell upon a patched Dunlop tyre. Up above us was the lighted window.

'I must have a peep through that, Watson. If you bend your back and support yourself upon the wall, I think that I can manage.'

'The Priory School'

September 6th

'Then there is the common error of making all the
characters stick or stock figures . . . We cannot be
adequately thrilled by a whole secret society who have
sworn to effect the death of a bore who is obviously
better dead. And even in order that the novelist should
kill people, it is first necessary that he should make
them live . . . We may very well add the general
principle that the most intense interest of a good
mystery story does not consist in incident at all. The
Sherlock Holmes stories are very good models of a
workmanlike type of popular mystery. And the point
of such a story is very seldom the story at all. The best
part of it is the comedy of the conversations between
Watson and Holmes.'

from 'Errors about Detective Stories'
by G. K. Chesterton

_____

_____

_____

_____

_____

_____

September 7th

'Well, it is just as I have been telling you, Mr Sherlock Holmes,' said Jabez Wilson, mopping his forehead. 'I have a small pawnbroker's business at Coburg Square, near the City. It's not a very large affair, and of late years it has not done more than just give me a living. I used to be able to keep two assistants, but now I only keep one; and I would have a job to pay him but that he is willing to come for half wages so as to learn the business.'

'The Red-Headed League'

_____

_____

_____

_____

September 8th

'Life is infinitely stranger than anything which the mind of man could invent. We would not dare to conceive the things which are really mere commonplaces of existence. If we could fly out of that window hand in hand, hover over this great city, gently remove the roofs and peep in at the queer things which are going on, the strange coincidences, the plannings, the cross-purposes, the wonderful chains of events, working through generations and leading to the most *outré* results, it would make all fiction with its conventionalities and foreseen conclusions most stale and unprofitable.'

Sherlock Holmes, *The Adventures of Sherlock Holmes*

September 9th

I came to the mantelpiece. A litter of pipes, tobacco-pouches, syringes, penknives, revolver-cartridges and other debris was scattered over it. In the midst of these was a small black and white ivory box with a sliding lid. It was a neat little thing, and I had stretched out my hand to examine it more closely when –

It was a dreadful cry that he gave – a yell which might have been heard down the street. My skin went cold and my hair bristled at that horrible scream. As I turned I caught a glimpse of a convulsed face and frantic eyes. I stood paralysed, with the little box in my hand.

'Put it down! Down, this instant, Watson – this instant, I say!'

'The Dying Detective'

_____

_____

_____

_____

_____

_____

September 10th

'[Sherlock Holmes] shows his powers by what the South Americans now call *Sherlockholmitos*, which means clever little deductions, which often have nothing to do with the matter in hand, but impress the reader with a general sense of power. The same effect is gained by his offhand allusion to other cases. Heaven knows how many titles I have thrown about in a casual way, and how many readers have begged me to satisfy their curiosity as to 'Rigoletto and His Abominable Wife', 'The Adventure of the Tired Captain' or 'The Curious Experience of the Patterson Family in the Island of Uffa'. Once or twice, as in 'The Adventure of the Second Stain', which in my judgement is one of the neatest of the stories, I did actually use the title years before I wrote a story to correspond.'

Memories and Adventures

September 11th

'But the underside is as stained as the upper. It must have left a mark.'

Lestrade chuckled with delight at having puzzled the famous expert.

'Now I'll show you the explanation. There *is* a second stain, but it does not correspond with the other. See for yourself.' As he spoke he turned over another portion of the carpet, and there, sure enough, was a great crimson spill upon the square white facing of the old-fashioned floor. 'What do you make of that, Mr Holmes?'

'The Second Stain'

_____

_____

_____

_____

_____

_____

_____

_____

September 12th

'I consider that a man's brain originally is like a little empty attic, and you have to stock it with such furniture as you choose. A fool takes in all the lumber of every sort that he comes across, so that the knowledge which might be useful to him gets crowded out, or at best is jumbled up with a lot of other things, so that he has a difficulty in laying his hands upon it. Now the skilled workman is very careful indeed as to what he takes into his brain-attic. He will have nothing but the tools which may help him in doing his work, but of these he has a large assortment, and all in the most perfect order. It is a mistake to think that that little room has elastic walls and can distend to any extent. Depend upon it there comes a time when for every addition of knowledge you forget something that you knew before. It is of the highest importance, therefore, not to have useless facts elbowing out the useful ones.'

Sherlock Holmes, *A Study in Scarlet*

_____

_____

_____

_____

_____

_____

September 13th

'Mr Warren is a timekeeper at Morton and Way-light's, in Tottenham Court Road. He has to be out of the house before seven. Well, this morning he had not gone ten paces down the road when two men came up behind him, threw a coat over his head, and bundled him into a cab that was beside the kerb. They drove him an hour, and then opened the door and shot him out. He lay in the roadway so shaken in his wits that he never saw what became of the cab. When he picked himself up he found he was on Hampstead Heath; so he took a bus home, and there he lies now on his sofa, while I came straight round to tell you what had happened.'

'The Red Circle'

September 14th

'Films of course were unknown when the stories appeared, and when these rights were finally discussed and a small sum offered for them by a French Company it seemed treasure trove and I was very glad to accept. Afterwards I had to buy them back again at exactly ten times what I had received, so the deal was a disastrous one. But now they have been done by the Stoll Company with Eille Norwood as Holmes, and it was worth all the expense to get so fine a production. Norwood . . . has the brooding eye which excites expectation and he has also a quite unrivalled power of disguise. My only criticism of the films is that they introduce telephones, motor cars and other luxuries of which the Victorian Holmes never dreamed.'

Memories and Adventures

_____

_____

_____

_____

_____

_____

_____

September 15th

Suddenly, as the landlady's footsteps died away, there was the creak of a turning key, the handle revolved, and two thin hands darted out and lifted the tray from the chair. An instant later it was hurriedly replaced, and I caught a glimpse of a dark, beautiful, horrified face glaring at the narrow opening of the boxroom. Then the door crashed to, the key turned once more, and all was silence. Holmes twitched my sleeve, and together we stole down the stair . . .

'The Red Circle'

273

September 16th

'His ignorance was as remarkable as his knowledge. Of contemporary literature, philosophy and politics he appeared to know next to nothing. Upon my quoting Thomas Carlyle, he enquired in the naïvest way who he might be and what he had done. My surprise reached a climax, however, when I found incidentally that he was ignorant of the Copernican Theory and of the composition of the Solar System. That any civilised human being in this nineteenth century should not be aware that the earth travelled round the sun appeared to me to be such an extra-ordinary fact that I could hardly realise it.'

Dr Watson, *A Study in Scarlet*

_____

_____

_____

_____

_____

_____

_____

_____

September 17th

'Perhaps not. That is why I thought it best to summon this lady to your aid.'

We all turned round at the words. There, framed in the doorway, was a tall and beautiful woman – the mysterious lodger of Bloomsbury. Slowly she advanced, her face pale and drawn with a frightful apprehension, her eyes fixed and staring, her terrified gaze riveted upon the dark figure on the floor.

'You have killed him!' she muttered. 'Oh, *Dio mio*, you have killed him!'

'The Red Circle'

_____

_____

_____

_____

_____

_____

_____

_____

_____

September 18th

'Sometimes I have got upon dangerous ground where I have taken risks through my own want of knowledge of the correct atmosphere . . . I read an excellent and very damaging criticism of "Silver Blaze" in some sporting paper, written clearly by a man who *did* know, in which he explained the exact penalties which would have come upon everyone concerned if they had acted as I described. Half would have been in jail and the other half warned off the turf for ever. However, I have never been nervous about details, and one must be masterful sometimes. When an alarmed editor wrote to me once: "There is no second line of rails at that point," I answered, "I make one." On the other hand, there are cases where accuracy is essential.'

Memories and Adventures

September 19th

'I went down as I had promised. When I reached the bridge she was waiting for me. Never did I realise till that moment how this poor creature hated me. She was like a mad woman – indeed, I think she *was* a mad woman, subtly mad with the deep power of deception which insane people sometimes have. How else could she have met me with unconcern every day and yet have so raging a hatred of me in her heart? I will not say what she said. She poured her whole wild fury out in burning and horrible words . . . '

'Thor Bridge'

September 20th

'I have no professional enquiry on foot at present. Hence the cocaine. I cannot live without brainwork. What else is there to live for? Stand at the window here. Was ever such a dreary, dismal, unprofitable world? See how the yellow fog swirls down the street and drifts across the dun-coloured houses. What could be more hopelessly prosaic and material? What is the use of having powers, doctor, when one has no field upon which to exert them? Crime is commonplace, existence is commonplace, and no qualities save those which are commonplace have any function upon earth.'

Sherlock Holmes, *The Sign of The Four*

September 21st

'But what could have caused it? Only great violence could have such an effect.'

Holmes did not answer. His pale, eager face had suddenly assumed that tense, faraway expression which I had learned to associate with the supreme manifestations of his genius . . . Suddenly he sprang from his chair, vibrating with nervous energy and the pressing need for action.

'Come, Watson, come!' he cried.

'Thor Bridge'

September 22nd

A story by Rudyard Kipling, 'The House Surgeon', concerning the investigation of a haunting, appeared in *Harper's Magazine* in 1909, and was seen as his Sherlock Holmes piece. The haunted house is called Homescroft, and the narrator-investigator says, 'I am less calculated to make a Sherlock Holmes than any man I know.' Conan Doyle and Kipling were neighbours in Sussex and they were old friends – although as time went by Kipling confessed to Rider Haggard that they had increasingly less in common. It is ironic that the story has a psychical theme, considering twenty years after it was written Doyle was to become a convinced Spiritualist.

September 23rd

'It was thick fog, and one could not see three yards. I had given two taps and Oberstein had come to the door. The young man rushed up and demanded to know what we were about to do with the papers. Oberstein had a short life-preserver. He always carried it with him. As West forced his way after us into the house Oberstein struck him on the head. The blow was a fatal one . . . There he lay in the hall, and we were at our wits' end what to do. Then Oberstein had this idea about the trains which halted under his back window . . . We waited half an hour at the window before a train stopped. It was so thick that nothing could be seen, and we had no difficulty in lowering West's body on to the train. That was the end of the matter so far as I was concerned.'

'The Bruce-Partington Plans'

September 24th

'The difficulty of the Holmes work was that every story really needed as clear-cut and original a plot as a longish book would do. One cannot without effort spin plots at such a rate. They are apt to become thin or to break. I was determined, now that I had no longer the excuse of absolute pecuniary pressure, never again to write anything which was not as good as I could possibly make it, and therefore I would not write a Holmes story without a worthy plot and without a problem which interested my own mind, for that is the first requisite before you can interest anyone else.'

Memories and Adventures

_____

_____

_____

_____

_____

_____

_____

_____

September 25th

With a shrill cry of anger a man rose from a reclining chair beside the fire. I saw a great yellow face, coarse-grained and greasy, with heavy double-chin, and two sullen, menacing grey eyes which glared at me from under tufted and sandy brows . . .

'What's this?' he cried in a high, screaming voice. 'What is the meaning of this intrusion? Didn't I send you word that I would see you tomorrow morning?'

'I am sorry,' said I, 'but the matter cannot be delayed. Mr Sherlock Holmes – '

The mention of my friend's name had an extraordinary effect upon the little man.

'The Dying Detective'

September 26th

'No, no: I never guess. It is a shocking habit – destructive to the logical faculty. What seems strange to you is only so because you do not follow my train of thought or observe the small facts upon which large inferences may depend. For example, I began by stating that your brother was careless. When you observe the lower part of that watch-case you notice that it is not only dinted in two places, but it is cut and marked all over from the habit of keeping other hard objects, such as coins or keys, in the same pocket. Surely it is no great feat to assume that a man who treats a fifty-guinea watch so cavalierly must be a careless man. Neither is it a very far-fetched inference that a man who inherits one article of such value is pretty well provided for in other respects.'

Sherlock Holmes, *The Sign of The Four*

September 27th

' "One must do something to ease an aching heart."
That was his own explanation. It was eccentric, no
doubt, but he is clearly an eccentric man. He tore up
one of his wife's photographs in my presence – tore it
up furiously in a tempest of passion. "I never wish to
see her damned face again," he shrieked.'

'The Retired Colourman'

_____

_____

_____

_____

_____

_____

_____

_____

_____

_____

_____

_____

September 28th

'If I have been able to sustain this character for a long time and if the public find, as they will find, that the last story is as good as the first, it is entirely due to the fact that I never, or hardly ever, forced a story. Some have thought there was a falling off in the stories [after the Reichenbach Falls]. I think, however, that if the reader began the series backwards, so that he brought a fresh mind to the last stories, he would agree with me that, though the general average may not be conspicuously high, still at least the same standard has been maintained.'

Memories and Adventures

September 29th

The situation was awkward, but the most direct way is often the best.

'Where is the Lady Frances Carfax?' I asked.

He stared at me with amazement.

'What have you done with her? Why have you pursued her? I insist upon an answer!' said I.

The fellow gave a bellow of anger and sprang upon me like a tiger. I have held my own in many a struggle, but the man had a grip of iron and the fury of a fiend. His hand was on my throat and my senses were nearly gone . . .

'The Disappearance of Lady Frances Carfax'

September 30th

'On one occasion while on a train to Sheffield I was thinking about my companion. It was one of Holmes's characteristics that he could command sleep at will. Unfortunately he could resist it at will also, and often and often have I had to remonstrate with him on the harm he must be doing himself when, deeply engrossed in one of his strange or baffling problems, he would go for several consecutive days and nights without one wink of sleep. He put the shades over the lamps, leant back in his corner and in less than two minutes his regular breathing told me was fast asleep . . . Now and again as we shot through some brilliantly illuminated station or past a line of flaming furnaces, I caught for an instant a glimpse of Holmes's figure coiled up snugly in the far corner with his head sunk upon his breast.'

Dr Watson, from 'The Man Who Was Wanted'
by Arthur Whitaker

OCTOBER

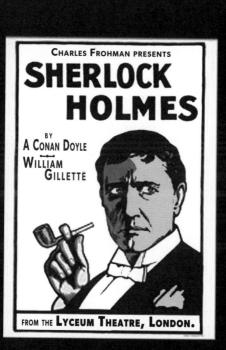

October 1st

'Another [correspondent] had a large amount of guile underlying her simplicity. Writing from Warsaw, she stated that she had been bedridden for two years, and that my novels had been her only, etc., etc. So touched was I by this flattering statement that I at once prepared an autographed parcel of them to complete the fair invalid's collection. By good luck, however, I met a brother author on the same day to whom I recounted the touching incident. With a cynical smile, he drew an identical letter from his pocket. His novels had also been for two years her only, etc., etc. I do not know how many more the lady had written to, but if, as I imagine, her correspondence had extended to several countries, she must have amassed a rather interesting library.'

Memories and Adventures

October 2nd

'I *mean* to find her,' said Sherlock Holmes. 'I'm going through this house till I do find her.'

'Where is your warrant?'

Holmes half drew a revolver from his pocket. 'This will have to serve till a better one comes.'

'Why, you're a common burglar.'

'So you might describe me,' said Holmes cheerfully. 'My companion is also a dangerous ruffian. And together we are going through your house.'

'The Disappearance of Lady Frances Carfax'

October 3rd

'It is simplicity itself . . . so absurdly simple that an explanation is superfluous; and yet it may serve to define the limits of observation and of deduction. Observation tells me that you have a little reddish mould adhering to your instep. Just opposite the Wigmore Street office they have taken up the pavement and thrown up some earth, which lies in such a way that it is difficult to avoid treading in it in entering. The earth is of this peculiar reddish tint which is found as far as I know nowhere else in the neighbourhood. So much is observation. The rest is deduction.'

Sherlock Holmes, *The Sign of The Four*

October 4th

At this moment we saw the man himself. His head showed above the edge of the cliff where the path ends. Then his whole figure appeared at the top, staggering like a drunken man. The next instant he threw up his hands, and, with a terrible cry, fell upon his face. Stackhurst and I rushed forward – it may have been fifty yards – and turned him on his back. He was obviously dying.

'The Lion's Mane'

October 5th

'There was one young lady who began all her epistles with the words "Good Lord" . . . The young Russian's habit of addressing me as "Good Lord" had an even stranger parallel at home . . . Shortly after I received a knighthood, I had a bill from a tradesman which was quite correct and businesslike in every detail save that it was made out to Sir Sherlock Holmes. I hope that I can stand a joke as well as my neighbours, but this particular piece of humour seemed rather misapplied and I wrote sharply upon the subject.'

Memories and Adventures

October 6th

The approach to the spot at which the tragedy occurred is down a narrow, winding, country lane. While we made our way along it we heard the rattle of a carriage coming towards us and stood aside to let it pass. As it drove by us I caught a glimpse through the closed window of a horribly contorted, grinning face glaring out at us. Those staring eyes and gnashing teeth flashed past us like a dreadful vision.

'The Devil's Foot'

_____

_____

_____

_____

_____

_____

_____

_____

_____

_____

October 7th

'Sherlock Holmes took his bottle from the corner of the mantelpiece and his hypodermic syringe from its neat morocco case. With his long, white, nervous fingers he adjusted the delicate needle and rolled back his left shirt-cuff. For some little time his eyes rested thoughtfully upon the sinewy forearm and wrist, all dotted and scarred with innumerable puncture-marks. Finally, he thrust the sharp point home, pressed down the tiny piston, and sank back into the velvet-lined armchair with a long sigh of satisfaction. Three times a day for many months I had witnessed this performance, but custom had not reconciled my mind to it.'

Dr Watson, *The Sign of The Four*

October 8th

We ascended the stairs and viewed the body. Miss Brenda Tregennis had been a very beautiful girl, though now verging upon middle age. Her dark, clear-cut face was handsome, even in death, but there still lingered upon it something of that convulsion of horror which had been her last human emotion.

'The Devil's Foot'

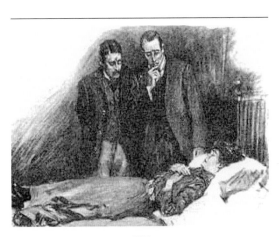

October 9th

'Sherlock Holmes was a man who seldom took exercise for exercise's sake. Few men were capable of greater muscular effort, and he was undoubtedly one of the finest boxers of his weight that I have ever seen; but he looked upon aimless bodily exertion as a waste of energy, and he seldom bestirred himself save when there was some professional object to be served. Then he was absolutely untiring and indefatigable. That he should have kept himself in training under such circumstances is remarkable, but his diet was usually of the sparest, and his habits were simple to the verge of austerity. Save for the occasional use of cocaine, he had no vices, and he only turned to the drug as a protest against the monotony of existence when cases were scanty and the papers uninteresting.'

Dr Watson, 'The Yellow Face'

_____

_____

_____

_____

_____

_____

_____

_____

October 10th

He had hardly spoken before there rushed into the room one of the most lovely young women that I have ever seen in my life. Her violet eyes shining, her lips parted, a pink flush upon her cheeks, all thought of her natural reserve was lost in her overpowering excitement and concern.

'Oh, Mr Sherlock Holmes!' she cried, glancing from one to the other of us, and finally, with a woman's quick intuition, fastening upon my companion. 'I am so glad that you have come. I have driven down to tell you so. I know that James didn't do it.'

'The Boscombe Valley Mystery'

October 11th

'I found the ash of a cigar, which my special know-ledge of tobacco ashes enables me to pronounce an Indian cigar. I have, as you know, devoted some attention to this, and written a little monograph on the ashes of one hundred and forty different varieties of pipe, cigar and cigarette tobacco. Having found the ash, I then looked round and discovered the stump among the moss where he had tossed it. It was an Indian cigar, of the variety which are rolled in Rotterdam . . . I could see that the end had not been in his mouth. Therefore he used a holder. The tip had been cut off, not bitten off, but the cut was not a clean one, so I deduced a blunt penknife.'

Sherlock Holmes, 'The Boscombe Valley Mystery'

_____

_____

_____

_____

_____

_____

_____

October 12th

' "Let me pass, I say!" He dashed her to one side, and, rushing to the window, cut at me with his heavy weapon. I had let myself go, and was hanging by my hands to the sill when his blow fell. I was conscious of a dull pain, my grip loosened, and I fell into the garden below.'

'The Engineer's Thumb'

October 13th

'You look at these scattered houses, and you are impressed by their beauty. I look at them, and the only thought which comes to me is a feeling of their isolation and of the impunity with which crime may be committed there . . . The pressure of public opinion can do in the town what the law cannot accomplish. There is no lane so vile that the scream of a tortured child or the thud of a drunkard's blow does not beget sympathy and indignation among the neighbours, and then the whole machinery of justice is ever so close that a word of complaint can set it going and there is but a step between the crime and the dock. But look at these lonely houses, each in its own fields, filled for the most part with poor ignorant folk who know little of the law. Think of the deeds of hellish cruelty, the hidden wickedness which may go on, year in, year out, in such places, and none the wiser.'

Holmes to Watson, 'The Copper Beeches'

October 14th

'There was an old chest of drawers in the room, the two upper ones empty and open, the lower one locked. I had filled the first two with my linen, and as I had still much to pack away I was naturally annoyed at not having the use of the third drawer. It struck me that it might have been fastened by a mere oversight, so I took out my bunch of keys and tried to open it. The very first key fitted to perfection, and I drew the drawer open. There was only one thing in it, but I am sure that you would never guess what it was . . . '

'The Copper Beeches'

October 15th

'There is nothing more deceptive than an obvious fact . . . To take the first example to hand, I very clearly perceive that in your bedroom the window is upon the right-hand side . . . '

'How on earth – '

'My dear fellow, I know you well. I know the military neatness which characterises you. You shave every morning, and in this season you shave by the sunlight; but since your shaving is less and less complete as we get farther back on the left side, until it becomes positively slovenly as we get round the angle of the jaw, it is surely very clear that that side is less illuminated than the other. I could not imagine a man of your habits looking at himself in an equal light and being satisfied with such a result. I only quote this as a trivial example of observation and inference. Therein lies my *métier* . . . '

Holmes and Watson, 'The Boscombe Valley
Mystery'

October 16th

Ryder threw himself down suddenly upon the rug and clutched at my companion's knees. 'For God's sake, have mercy!' he shrieked. 'Think of my father! Of my mother! It would break their hearts. I never went wrong before! I never will again. I swear it. I'll swear it on a Bible. Oh, don't bring it into court! For Christ's sake, don't!'

'The Blue Carbuncle'

October 17th

'The vocabulary of *Bradshaw* is nervous and terse, but limited. The selection of words would hardly lend itself to the sending of general messages. We will eliminate *Bradshaw* . . . Let us consider the claims of *Whitaker's Almanac* . . . Though reserved in its earlier vocabulary, it becomes, if I remember right, quite garrulous towards the end . . . Here is page 534, column two, a substantial block of print dealing, I perceive, with the trade and resources of British India. Jot down the words, Watson! Number thirteen is "Mahratta". Not, I fear, a very auspicious beginning. Number one hundred and twenty-seven is "Government"; which at least makes sense, though somewhat irrelevant to ourselves and Professor Moriarty. Now let us try again. What does the Mahratta government do? Alas! the next word is "pig's-bristles". We are undone, my good Watson! It is finished!'

Sherlock Holmes, *The Valley of Fear*

October 18th

'Today I was not alarmed, but I was filled with curiosity, and I determined to find out who he was and what he wanted. I slowed down my machine, but he slowed down his. Then I stopped altogether, but he stopped also. Then I laid a trap for him. There is a sharp turning of the road, and I pedalled very quickly round this, and then I stopped and waited. I expected him to shoot round and pass me before he could stop. But he never appeared. Then I went back and looked round the corner. I could see a mile of road, but he was not on it. To make it the more extraordinary, there was no side road at this point down which he could have gone.'

'The Solitary Cyclist'

October 19th

'I have already explained to you that what is out of the common is usually a guide rather than a hindrance. In solving a problem of this sort, the grand thing is to be able to reason backwards. That is a very useful accomplishment, and a very easy one, but people do not practise it much. In the everyday affairs of life it is more useful to reason forwards, and so the other comes to be neglected. There are fifty who can reason synthetically for one who can reason analytically . . . Most people, if you describe a train of events to them, will tell you what the result would be. They can put those events together in their minds, and argue from them that something will come to pass. There are few people, however, who, if you told them a result, would be able to evolve from their own inner consciousness what the steps were which led up to that result. This power is what I mean when I talk of reasoning backwards, or analytically.'

Sherlock Holmes, *A Study in Scarlet*

October 20th

In half an hour, we were clear of the town and hastening down a country road.

'What have you done, Holmes?' I asked.

'A threadbare and venerable device, but useful upon occasion. I walked into the doctor's yard this morning and shot my syringe full of aniseed over the hind wheel. A draghound will follow aniseed from here to John o' Groats, and our friend Armstrong would have to drive through the Cam before he would shake Pompey off his trail.'

'The Missing Three-Quarter'

October 21st

'Mediocrity knows nothing higher than itself; but talent instantly recognises genius. MacDonald had talent enough for his profession to enable him to perceive that there was no humiliation in seeking the assistance of one who already stood alone in Europe, both in his gifts and in his experience. Holmes was not prone to friendship, but he was tolerant of the big Scotchman, and smiled at the sight of him . . . It was one of those dramatic moments for which my friend existed. It would be an overstatement to say that he was shocked or even excited by [MacDonald's] amazing announcement. Without having a tinge of cruelty in his singular composition, he was un-doubtedly callous from long over-stimulation. Yet, if his emotions were dulled, his intellectual perceptions were exceedingly active.'

Dr Watson, *The Valley of Fear*

October 22nd

So tall was he that his hat actually brushed the cross-bar of the doorway, and his breadth seemed to span it across from side to side. A large face, seared with a thousand wrinkles, burned yellow by the sun and marked with every evil passion, was turned from one to the other of us, while his deep-set, bile-shot eyes and his high, thin, fleshless nose gave him somewhat the resemblance to a fierce old bird of prey . . .

'I know you, you scoundrel! I have heard of you before. You are Holmes, the meddler.'

'The Speckled Band'

October 23rd

'My friend rose lazily from his armchair and stood with his hands in the pockets of his dressing-gown, looking over my shoulder. It was a bright, crisp February morning, and the snow of the day before still lay deep upon the ground, shimmering brightly in the wintry sun. Down the centre of Baker Street it had been ploughed into a brown crumbly band by the traffic, but at either side and on the heaped-up edges of the footpaths it still lay as white as when it fell. The grey pavement had been cleaned and scraped, but was still dangerously slippery, so that there were fewer passengers than usual. Indeed, from the direction of the Metropolitan Line station no one was coming save the single gentleman whose eccentric conduct had drawn my attention.'

Dr Watson, 'The Beryl Coronet'

October 24th

'... Is it madness, Mr Holmes? Is it something in the blood? Have you any similar case in your experience? For God's sake, give me some advice, for I am at my wits' end.'

'Very naturally, Mr Ferguson. Now sit here and pull yourself together and give me a few clear answers. I can assure you that I am very far from being at my wits' end, and that I am confident we shall find some solution. First of all, tell me what steps you have taken. Is your wife still near the children?'

'The Sussex Vampire'

October 25th

'Holmes, who loathed every form of society with his whole Bohemian soul, remained in our lodgings in Baker Street, buried among his old books, and alternating from week to week between cocaine and ambition, the drowsiness of the drug and the fierce energy of his own keen nature. He was still, as ever, deeply attracted by the study of crime, and occupied his immense faculties and extraordinary powers of observation in following out those clues and clearing up those mysteries which had been abandoned as hopeless by the official police. From time to time I heard some vague account of his doings: of his summons to Odessa in the case of the Trepoff murder, of his clearing up of the singular tragedy of the Atkinson brothers at Trincomalee and, finally, of the mission which he had accomplished so delicately and successfully for the reigning family of Holland. Beyond these signs of his activity, however, which I merely shared with all the readers of the daily press, I knew little of my former friend and companion.'

Dr Watson, 'A Scandal in Bohemia'

October 26th

Our thoughts were entirely absorbed by the terrible object which lay upon the tiger-skin hearthrug in front of the fire.

'The Abbey Grange'

October 27th

'I was seized with a keen desire to see Holmes again, and to know how he was employing his extraordinary powers. His rooms were brilliantly lit and, even as I looked up, I saw his tall, spare figure pass twice in dark silhouette against the blind. He was pacing the room swiftly, eagerly, with his head sunk upon his chest and his hands clasped behind him. To me, who knew his every mood and habit, his attitude and manner told their own story. He was at work again. He had risen out of his drug-created dreams and was hot upon the scent of some new problem.'

Dr Watson, 'A Scandal in Bohemia'

October 28th

'Come in, Sherlock! Come in, sir,' said he blandly, smiling at our surprised faces. 'You don't expect such energy from me, do you, Sherlock? But somehow this case attracts me.'

'The Greek Interpreter'

October 29th

'Glancing over the somewhat incoherent series of memoirs with which I have endeavoured to illustrate a few of the mental peculiarities of my friend Mr Sherlock Holmes, I have been struck by the difficulty which I have experienced in picking out examples which shall in every way answer my purpose. For in those cases in which Holmes has performed some *tour de force* of analytical reasoning, and has demonstrated the value of his peculiar methods of investigation, the facts themselves have often been so slight or so commonplace that I could not feel justified in laying them before the public. On the other hand, it has frequently happened that he has been concerned in some research where the facts have been of the most remarkable and dramatic character, but where the share which he has himself taken in determining their causes has been less pronounced than I, as his biographer, could wish.'

Dr Watson, 'The Resident Patient'

October 30th

It had been a close, rainy day in October. 'Unhealthy weather, Watson,' said my friend. 'But the evening has brought a breeze with it. What do you say to a ramble through London?'

I was weary of our little sitting-room and gladly acquiesced. For three hours we strolled about together, watching the ever-changing kaleidoscope of life as it ebbs and flows through Fleet Street and the Strand. Holmes's characteristic talk, with its keen observance of detail and subtle power of inference, held me amused and enthralled.

'The Resident Patient'

October 31st

'An anomaly which often struck me in the character of my friend Sherlock Holmes was that, although in his methods of thought he was the neatest and most methodical of mankind, and although also he affected a certain quiet primness of dress, he was none the less in his personal habits one of the most untidy men that ever drove a fellow-lodger to distraction. Not that I am in the least conventional in that respect myself. The rough-and-tumble work in Afghanistan, coming on the top of a natural Bohemianism of disposition, has made me rather more lax than befits a medical man. But with me there is a limit, and when I find a man who keeps his cigars in the coal-scuttle, his tobacco in the toe end of a Persian slipper, and his unanswered correspondence transfixed by a jackknife into the very centre of his wooden mantelpiece, then I begin to give myself virtuous airs.'

Dr Watson, 'The Musgrave Ritual'

NOVEMBER

November 1st

'I have always held, too, that pistol practice should be distinctly an open-air pastime; and when Holmes, in one of his queer humours, would sit in an armchair with his hair-trigger and a hundred Boxer cartridges, and proceed to adorn the opposite wall with a patriotic VR done in bullet-pocks, I felt strongly that neither the atmosphere nor the appearance of our room was improved by it. Our chambers were always full of chemicals and of criminal relics which had a way of wandering into unlikely positions, and of turning up in the butter-dish or in even less desirable places.'

Dr Watson, 'The Musgrave Ritual'

November 2nd

'But what next, Mr Holmes?'

'Well, then came an incident which was rather unexpected to myself. I was slipping through the pantry window in the early dawn when I felt a hand inside my collar, and a voice said: "Now, you rascal, what are you doing in there?" When I could twist my head round I looked into the tinted spectacles of my friend and rival, Mr Barker.'

'The Retired Colourman'

November 3rd

'But his papers were my great crux. He had a horror of destroying documents, especially those which were connected with his past cases, and yet it was only once in every year or two that he would muster energy to docket and arrange them; for, as I have mentioned somewhere in these incoherent memoirs, the outbursts of passionate energy when he performed the remarkable feats with which his name is associated were followed by reactions of lethargy during which he would lie about with his violin and his books, hardly moving save from the sofa to the table. Thus month after month his papers accumulated, until every corner of the room was stacked with bundles of manuscript which were on no account to be burned, and which could not be put away save by their owner.'

Dr Watson, 'The Musgrave Ritual'

_____

_____

_____

_____

_____

_____

November 4th

'Every enquiry in this case reveals something inexplicable. Now there are three papers still missing. They are, as I understand, the vital ones.'

'Yes, that is so.'

'Do you mean to say that anyone holding these three papers, and without the seven others, could construct a Bruce-Partington submarine?'

'The Bruce-Partington Papers'

November 5th

'During my long and intimate acquaintance with Mr Sherlock Holmes I had never heard him refer to his relations, and hardly ever to his own early life. This reticence upon his part had increased the somewhat inhuman effect which he produced upon me, until sometimes I found myself regarding him as an isolated phenomenon, a brain without a heart, as deficient in human sympathy as he was pre-eminent in intelligence. His aversion to women and his disinclination to form new friendships were both typical of his unemotional character, but not more so than his complete suppression of every reference to his own people.'

Dr Watson, 'The Greek Interpreter'

_____

_____

_____

_____

_____

_____

_____

November 6th

Mycroft Holmes was a much larger and stouter man than Sherlock. His body was absolutely corpulent, but his face, though massive, had preserved something of the sharpness of expression which was so remarkable in that of his brother. His eyes, which were of a peculiarly light, watery grey, seemed always to retain that faraway, introspective look which I had only observed in Sherlock's when he was exerting his full powers.

'The Greek Interpreter'

November 7th

'It was indeed like old times when, at that hour, I found myself seated beside him in a hansom, my revolver in my pocket and the thrill of adventure in my heart. Holmes was cold and stern and silent. As the gleam of the street-lamps flashed upon his austere features I saw that his brows were drawn down in thought and his thin lips compressed. I knew not what wild beast we were about to hunt down in the dark jungle of criminal London, but I was well assured from the bearing of this master huntsman that the adventure was a most grave one, while the sardonic smile which occasionally broke through his ascetic gloom boded little good for the object of our quest.'

Dr Watson, 'The Empty House'

_____

_____

_____

_____

_____

_____

_____

November 8th

'I should say that there is no more dangerous man in Europe.'

'I have had several opponents to whom that flattering term has been applied,' said Holmes, with a smile . . . 'If your man is more dangerous than the late Professor Moriarty, or than the living Colonel Sebastian Moran, then he is indeed worth meeting. May I ask his name?'

'Have you ever heard of Baron Gruner?'

'You mean the Austrian murderer?'

Colonel Damery threw up his kid-gloved hands with a laugh. 'There is no getting past you, Mr Holmes! Wonderful! So you have already sized him up as a murderer?'

'The Illustrious Client'

November 9th

'You see, my dear Watson' – he propped his test-tube in the rack and began to lecture with the air of a professor addressing his class – 'it is not really difficult to construct a series of inferences, each dependent upon its predecessor and each simple in itself. If, after doing so, one simply knocks out all the central inferences and presents one's audience with the starting-point and the conclusion, one may produce a startling, though possibly a meretricious, effect. Now, it was not really difficult, by an inspection of the groove between your left forefinger and thumb, to feel sure that you did *not* propose to invest your small capital in the goldfields.'

Sherlock Holmes, 'The Dancing Men'

_____

_____

_____

_____

_____

_____

_____

November 10th

'Look at that with your magnifying glass, Mr Holmes.'

'Yes, I am doing so.'

'You are aware that no two thumb marks are alike?'

'I have heard something of the kind.'

'Well, then, will you please compare that print with this wax impression of young McFarlane's right thumb, taken by my orders this morning?'

'The Norwood Builder'

November 11th

'Holmes like all great artists, lived for his art's sake, and, I have seldom known him claim any large reward for his inestimable services. So unworldly was he – or so capricious – that he frequently refused his help to the powerful and wealthy where the problem made no appeal to his sympathies, while he would devote weeks of most intense application to the affairs of some humble client whose case presented those strange and dramatic qualities which appealed to his imagination and challenged his ingenuity.'

Dr Watson, 'Black Peter'

November 12th

'Good-day, Lord St Simon,' said Holmes, rising and bowing. 'Pray take the basket-chair. This is my friend and colleague, Dr Watson. Draw up a little to the fire, and we will talk this matter over.'

'A most painful matter to me, as you can most readily imagine, Mr Holmes. I have been cut to the quick. I understand that you have already managed several delicate cases of this sort, sir, though I presume that they were hardly from the same class of society.'

'No, I am descending.'

'I beg pardon.'

'My last client of the sort was a king.'

'The Noble Bachelor'

_____

_____

_____

_____

_____

_____

November 13th

'Somewhere in the vaults of the bank of Cox and Co., at Charing Cross, there is a travel-worn and battered tin dispatch-box with my name, John H. Watson, MD, Late Indian Army, painted upon the lid. It is crammed with papers, nearly all of which are records of cases to illustrate the curious problems which Mr Sherlock Holmes had at various times to examine . . . Among these unfinished tales is that of Mr James Phillimore, who, stepping back into his own house to get his umbrella, was never more seen in this world. No less remarkable is that of the cutter *Alicia*, which sailed one spring morning into a small patch of mist from which she never again emerged . . . A third case worthy of note is that of Isadore Persano, the well-known journalist and duellist, who was found stark staring mad with a matchbox in front of him which contained a remarkable worm, said to be unknown to science.'

Dr Watson, 'Thor Bridge'

November 14th

The man sprang to his feet with a hoarse scream. He clawed the air with his bony hands. His mouth was open and for the instant he looked like some horrible bird of prey. In a flash we got a glimpse of the real Josiah Amberley, a misshapen demon with a soul as distorted as his body. As he fell back into his chair he clapped his hand to his lips as if to stifle a cough. Holmes sprang at his throat like a tiger, and twisted his face towards the ground. A white pellet fell from between his gasping lips.

'The Retired Colourman'

November 15th

'When one considers that Mr Sherlock Holmes was in active practice for twenty-three years, and that during seventeen of these I was allowed to co-operate with him and to keep notes of his doings, it will be clear that I have a mass of material at my command. The problem has always been not to find but to choose. There is the long row of year-books which fill a shelf, and there are the dispatch-cases filled with documents, a perfect quarry for the student not only of crime but of the social and official scandals of the late Victorian era. Concerning these latter, I may say that the writers of agonised letters, who beg that the honour of their families or the reputation of famous forbears may not be touched, have nothing to fear. The discretion and high sense of professional honour which have always distinguished my friend are still at work.'

Dr Watson, 'The Veiled Lodger'

November 16th

The woman stood with her hand buried in her bosom, and the same deadly smile on her thin lips.

'You will ruin no more lives as you ruined mine. You will wring no more hearts as you wrung mine. I will free the world of a poisonous thing. Take that, you hound, and that! – and that! – and that!'

She had drawn a little gleaming revolver, and emptied barrel after barrel into Milverton's body, the muzzle within two feet of his shirt front.

'Charles Augustus Milverton'

November 17th

'It was a wild morning in October, and I observed as I was dressing how the last remaining leaves were being whirled from the solitary plane tree which graces the yard behind our house. I descended to breakfast prepared to find my companion in depressed spirits, for, like all great artists, he was easily impressed by his surroundings. On the contrary, I found that he had nearly finished his meal, and that his mood was particularly bright and joyous, with that somewhat sinister cheerfulness which was characteristic of his lighter moments.

' "You have a case, Holmes?" I remarked.

' "The faculty of deduction is certainly contagious, Watson," he answered. "It has enabled you to probe my secret. Yes, I have a case. After a month of trivialities and stagnation the wheels move once more." '

Dr Watson, 'Thor Bridge'

November 18th

'Come, come,' said Holmes, kindly; 'it is human to err, and at least no one can accuse you of being a callous criminal. Perhaps it would be easier for you if I were to tell Mr Soames what occurred, and you can check me where I am wrong. Shall I do so? Well, well, don't trouble to answer. Listen, and see that I do you no injustice.

'From the moment, Mr Soames, that you said to me that no one, not even Bannister, could have told that the papers were in your room, the case began to take a definite shape in my mind.'

'The Three Students'

November 19th

'Things had indeed been very slow with us, and I had learned to dread such periods of inaction, for I knew by experience that my companion's brain was so abnormally active that it was dangerous to leave it without material upon which to work. For years I had gradually weaned him from that drug mania which had threatened once to check his remarkable career. Now I knew that under ordinary conditions he no longer craved for this artificial stimulus, but I was well aware that the fiend was not dead, but sleeping; and I have known that the sleep was a light one and the waking near when in periods of idleness I have seen the drawn look upon Holmes's ascetic face, and the brooding of his deep-set and inscrutable eyes.'

Dr Watson in 'The Missing Three-Quarter'

_____

_____

_____

_____

_____

_____

_____

_____

November 20th

'Hum!' said Holmes, 'have you got his cigar-holder?'

'No, I have seen none.'

'His cigar-case, then?'

'Yes, it was in his coat-pocket.'

Holmes opened it and smelled the single cigar which it contained.

'Oh, this is a Havana, and these others are cigars of the peculiar sort which are imported by the Dutch from their East Indian colonies.'

'The Resident Patient'

November 21st

'All life is a great chain, the nature of which is known wherever we are shown a single link of it. Like all other arts, the science of deduction and analysis is one which can only be acquired by long and patient study, nor is life long enough to allow any mortal to attain the highest possible perfection in it. Before turning to those moral and mental aspects of the matter which present the greatest difficulties, let the enquirer begin by mastering more elementary problems . . . By a man's fingernails, by his coat-sleeve, by his boot, by his trouser-knees, by the callosities of his forefinger and thumb, by his expression, by his shirt-cuffs – by each of these things a man's calling is plainly revealed. That all united should fail to enlighten the competent enquirer in any case is almost inconceivable.

Sherlock Holmes, 'A Study in Scarlet'

November 22nd

During our return journey I could see by Holmes's face that he was much puzzled by something which he had observed . . . At last, by a sudden impulse, just as our train was crawling out of a suburban station, he sprang on to the platform and pulled me out after him. 'Excuse me, my dear fellow,' said he, as we watched the rear carriages of our train disappearing round a curve; 'I am sorry to make you the victim of what may seem a mere whim, but on my life, Watson, I simply *can't* leave that case in this condition.'

'The Abbey Grange'

November 23rd

'I must admit, Watson, that you have some power of selection which atones for much that I deplore in your narratives. Your fatal habit of looking at everything from the point of view of a story instead of as a scientific exercise has ruined what might have been an instructive and even classical series of demonstrations. You slur over work of the utmost finesse and delicacy in order to dwell upon sensational details which may excite, but cannot possibly instruct, the reader.'

'Why do you not write them yourself?' I said, with some bitterness.

'I will, my dear Watson, I will. At present I am, as you know, fairly busy, but I propose to devote my declining years to the composition of a textbook which shall focus the whole art of detection into one volume.'

Holmes and Watson, 'The Abbey Grange'

November 24th

'The passage was dark save that one window halfway along it threw a patch of light. I could see that something was coming along the passage, something dark and crouching. Then suddenly it emerged into the light, and I saw that it was he. He was crawling, Mr Holmes – crawling! He was not quite on his hands and knees. I should rather say on his hands and feet, with his face sunk between his hands. Yet he seemed to move with ease. I was so paralysed by the sight that it was not until he had reached my door that I was able to step forward and ask if I could assist him.'

'The Creeping Man'

November 25th

'In choosing a few typical cases which illustrate the remarkable mental qualities of my friend, Sherlock Holmes, I have endeavoured, as far as possible, to select those which presented the minimum of sensationalism, while offering a fair field for his talents. It is, however, unfortunately impossible entirely to separate the sensational from the criminal, and a chronicler is left in the dilemma that he must either sacrifice details which are essential to his statement and so give a false impression of the problem, or he must use matter which chance, and not choice, has provided him with.'

Dr Watson 'The Cardboard Box'

November 26th

For all the preposterous hat and the vacuous face, there was something noble in the simple faith of our visitor which compelled our respect. She laid her little bundle of papers upon the table and went her way, with a promise to come again whenever she might be summoned.

Sherlock Holmes sat silent for a few minutes with his fingertips still pressed together, his legs stretched out in front of him, and his gaze directed upward to the ceiling.

'A Case of Identity'

_____

_____

_____

_____

_____

_____

_____

_____

_____

November 27th

'In the third week of November a dense yellow fog settled down upon London. From the Monday to the Thursday I doubt whether it was ever possible from our windows in Baker Street to see the loom of the opposite houses. The first day Holmes had spent in cross-indexing his huge book of references. The second and third had been patiently occupied upon a subject which he had recently made his hobby – the music of the Middle Ages. But when, for the fourth time, after pushing back our chairs from breakfast we saw the greasy, heavy brown swirl still drifting past us and condensing in oily drops upon the windowpanes, my comrade's impatient and active nature could endure this drab existence no longer. He paced restlessly about our sitting-room in a fever of suppressed energy, biting his nails, tapping the furniture, and chafing against inaction.'

Dr Watson, 'The Bruce-Partington Papers'

November 28th

A few moments later he was in our room, still puffing, still gesticulating, but with so fixed a look of grief and despair in his eyes that our smiles were turned in an instant to horror and pity. For a while he could not get his words out, but swayed his body and plucked at his hair like one who has been driven to the extreme limits of his reason . . .

'No doubt you think me mad?' said he.

'The Beryl Coronet'

_____

_____

_____

November 29th

'One of the most remarkable characteristics of Sherlock Holmes was his power of throwing his brain out of action and switching all his thoughts on to lighter things whenever he had convinced himself that he could no longer work to advantage. I remember that during the whole of that memorable day he lost himself in a monograph which he had undertaken upon the Polyphonic Motets of Lassus. For my own part I had none of this power of detachment, and the day, in consequence, appeared to be interminable.'

Dr Watson, 'The Bruce-Partington Papers'

November 30th

'These last words were in Greek, and at the same instant the man with a convulsive effort tore the plaster from his lips, and screaming out "Sophy! Sophy!" rushed into the woman's arms. Their embrace was but for an instant, however, for the younger man seized the woman and pushed her out of the room, while the elder easily overpowered his emaciated victim, and dragged him away through the other door.'

'The Greek Interpreter'

_____

_____

_____

_____

_____

_____

_____

_____

_____

DECEMBER

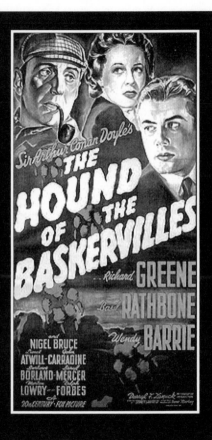

December 1st

He stopped suddenly and stared fixedly up over my head into the air. The lamp beat upon his face, and so intent was it and so still that it might have been that of a clear-cut classical statue, a personification of alertness and expectation.

The Hound of the Baskervilles

December 2nd

'Mrs Hudson, the landlady of Sherlock Holmes, was a long-suffering woman. Not only was her first-floor flat invaded at all hours by throngs of singular and often undesirable characters, but her remarkable lodger showed an eccentricity and irregularity in his life which must have sorely tried her patience. His incredible untidiness, his addiction to music at strange hours, his occasional revolver practice within doors, his weird and often malodorous scientific experiments, and the atmosphere of violence and danger which hung around him made him the very worst tenant in London. On the other hand, his payments were princely. I have no doubt that the house might have been purchased at the price which Holmes paid for his rooms during the years that I was with him.'

Dr Watson, 'The Dying Detective'

December 3rd

He turned and tore open the coffin-lid behind him. In the glare of the lantern I saw a body swathed in a sheet from head to foot, with dreadful, witch-like features, all nose and chin, projecting at one end, the dim, glazed eyes staring from a discoloured and crumbling face. The baronet had staggered back with a cry and supported himself against a stone sarcophagus.

'Shoscombe Old Place'

December 4th

'His powers upon the violin were very remarkable, but as eccentric as all his other accomplishments. That he could play pieces, and difficult pieces, I knew well, because at my request he had played me some of Mendelssohn's *Lieder*, and other favourites. When left to himself, however, he would seldom produce any music or attempt any recognised air. Leaning back in his armchair of an evening, he would close his eyes and scrape carelessly at the fiddle which was thrown across his knee. Sometimes the chords were sonorous and melancholy. Occasionally they were fantastic and cheerful. Clearly they reflected the thoughts which possessed him, but whether the music aided those thoughts, or whether the playing was simply the result of a whim or fancy, was more than I could determine. I might have rebelled against these exasperating solos had it not been that he usually terminated them by playing in quick succession a whole series of my favourite airs as a slight compensation for the trial upon my patience.'

Dr Watson, *A Study in Scarlet*

December 5th

'I shall try over the Hoffmann Barcarolle upon my
violin. In five minutes I shall return for your final
answer. You quite grasp the alternative, do you not?
Shall we take you, or shall we have the stone?'

Holmes withdrew, picking up his violin from the
corner as he passed. A few moments later the long-
drawn, wailing notes of that most haunting of tunes
came faintly through the closed door of the bedroom.

'The Mazarin Stone'

December 6th

'I had begun to think that my companion was as friendless a man as I was myself. Presently, however, I found that he had many acquaintances, and those in the most different classes of society. There was one little sallow, rat-faced, dark-eyed fellow, who was introduced to me as Mr Lestrade, and who came three or four times in a single week. When any of these nondescript individuals put in an appearance Sherlock Holmes used to beg for the use of the sitting-room and I would retire to my bedroom. He always apologised to me for putting me to this inconvenience. "I have to use this room as a place of business," he said, "and these people are my clients." '

Dr Watson, *A Study in Scarlet*

December 7th

There was a sudden rush and a scuffle, followed by the clash of iron and a cry of pain.

'You'll only get yourself hurt,' said the inspector. 'Stand still, will you?' There was the click of the closing handcuffs.

'A nice trap!' cried the high, snarling voice. 'It will bring *you* into the dock, Holmes, not me.'

'The Dying Detective'

_____

_____

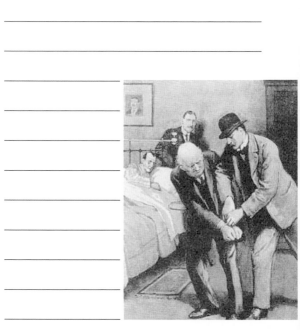

December 8th

It was a blazing hot day in August. Baker Street was like an oven, and the glare of the sunlight upon the yellow brickwork of the house across the road was painful to the eye. It was hard to believe that these were the same walls which loomed so gloomily through the fogs of winter . . . Parliament had risen. Everybody was out of town, and I yearned for the glades of the New Forest or the shingle of Southsea, [but] neither the country nor the sea presented the slightest attraction to him. He loved to lie in the very centre of five millions of people, with his filaments stretching out and running through them, responsive to every little rumour or suspicion of unsolved crime. Appreciation of nature found no place among his many gifts, and his only change was when he turned his mind from the evildoer of the town to track down his brother of the country.

Dr Watson, 'The Cardboard Box'

_____

_____

_____

_____

_____

_____

December 9th

He had gone out before breakfast, and I had sat down to mine, when he strode into the room, his hat upon his head and a huge barbed-headed spear tucked like an umbrella under his arm.

'Good gracious, Holmes!' I cried. 'You don't mean to say that you have been walking about London with that thing?'

'Black Peter'

December 10th

'In recording from time to time some of the curious experiences and interesting recollections which I associate with my long and intimate friendship with Mr Sherlock Holmes, I have continually been faced by difficulties caused by his own aversion to publicity. To his sombre and cynical spirit all popular applause was always abhorrent, and nothing amused him more at the end of a successful case than to hand over the actual exposure to some orthodox official, and to listen with a mocking smile to the general chorus of misplaced congratulation . . . My participation in some of his adventures was always a privilege which entailed discretion and reticence upon me.'

Dr Watson, 'The Devil's Foot'

December 11th

Lady Frances found her comfort and occupation in religion. Dr Shlessinger's remarkable personality, his wholehearted devotion, and the fact that he was recovering from a disease contracted in the exercise of his apostolic duties, affected her deeply. She had helped Mrs Shlessinger in the nursing of the convalescent saint. He spent his day, as the manager described it to me, upon a lounge-chair on the veranda, with an attendant lady upon either side of him.

'The Disappearance of Lady Frances Carfax'

December 12th

'You remind me of Edgar Allan Poe's Dupin. I had no idea that such individuals did exist outside of stories.'

Sherlock Holmes rose and lit his pipe. 'No doubt you think that you are complimenting me in comparing me to Dupin,' he observed. 'Now, in my opinion, Dupin was a very inferior fellow.' . . .

'Have you read Gaboriau's works?' I asked. 'Does Lecoq come up to your idea of a detective?'

Sherlock Holmes sniffed sardonically. 'Lecoq was a miserable bungler,' he said, in an angry voice . . .

I felt rather indignant at having two characters whom I had admired treated in this cavalier style. I walked over to the window, and stood looking out into the busy street. 'This fellow may be very clever,' I said to myself, 'but he is certainly very conceited.'

Watson and Holmes, *A Study in Scarlet*

December 13th

We had risen to go, but there was something in the woman's voice which arrested Holmes's attention. He turned swiftly upon her.

'Your life is not your own,' he said. 'Keep your hands off it.'

'What use is it to anyone?'

'How can you tell? The example of patient suffering is in itself the most precious of all lessons to an impatient world.'

The woman's answer was a terrible one. She raised her veil and stepped forward into the light.

'I wonder if you would bear it,' she said.

'The Veiled Lodger'

December 14th

'The ideas of my friend Watson, though limited, are exceedingly pertinacious. For a long time he has worried me to write an experience of my own. Perhaps I have rather invited this persecution, since I have often had occasion to point out to him how superficial are his own accounts and to accuse him of pandering to popular taste instead of confining himself rigidly to fact and figures. "Try it yourself, Holmes!" he has retorted, and I am compelled to admit that, having taken my pen in my hand, I do begin to realise that the matter must be presented in such a way as may interest the reader.'

Sherlock Holmes, 'The Blanched Soldier'

_____

_____

_____

_____

_____

_____

_____

_____

December 15th

Colonel Emsworth pointed to me.

'This is the gentleman who forced my hand.' He unfolded the scrap of paper on which I had written the word 'Leprosy'. 'It seemed to me that if he knew so much as that it was safer that he should know all.'

'The Blanched Soldier'

———————————————————

———————————————————

———————————————————

———————————————————

———————————————————

December 16th

'We were in our rooms in Baker Street one evening. I was, I remember, by the centre table writing out 'The Adventure of the Man Without a Cork Leg' (which had so puzzled the Royal Society and all the other scientific bodies of Europe), and Holmes was amusing himself with a little revolver practice. It was his custom of a summer evening to fire round my head, just shaving my face, until he had made a photograph of me on the opposite wall, and it is a slight proof of his skill that many of these portraits in pistol shots are considered admirable likenesses.'

from J. M. Barrie's friendly parody
'The Adventure of the Two Collaborators'

_____

_____

_____

_____

_____

_____

_____

_____

December 17th

Both Holmes and I had a weakness for the Turkish Bath. It was over a smoke in the pleasant lassitude of the drying-room that I found him less reticent and more human than anywhere else. On the upper floor of the Northumberland Avenue establishment there is an isolated corner where two couches lie side by side . . . I had asked him whether anything was stirring, and for answer he had shot his long, thin, nervous arm out of the sheets which enveloped him and had drawn an envelope from the inside pocket of the coat which hung beside him.

'The Illustrious Client'

December 18th

It was pleasant to Dr Watson to find himself once more in the untidy room of the first floor in Baker Street which had been the starting point of so many remarkable adventures. He looked round him at the scientific charts upon the wall, the acid-charred bench of chemicals, the violin-case leaning in the corner, the coal-scuttle, which contained of old the pipes and tobacco. Finally, his eyes came round to the fresh and smiling face of Billy, the young but very wise and tactful page, who had helped a little to fill up the gap of loneliness and isolation which surrounded the saturnine figure of the great detective.

Conan Doyle, 'The Mazarin Stone'

December 19th

'I had hoped,' suggested Holmes, 'that you would have joined us in a friendly supper.'

'I think that there you ask a little too much,' responded his lordship. 'I may be forced to acquiesce in these recent developments, but I can hardly be expected to make merry over them. I think that with your permission I will now wish you all a very good-night.' He included us all in a sweeping bow and stalked out of the room.

'The Noble Bachelor'

December 20th

'When I look at the three massive manuscript volumes which contain our work for the year 1894, I confess that it is very difficult for me, out of such a wealth of material, to select the cases which are most interesting in themselves and at the same time most conducive to a display of those peculiar powers for which my friend was famous. As I turn over the pages I see my notes upon the repulsive story of the red leech and the terrible death of Crosby the banker. Here also I find an account of the Addleton tragedy and the singular contents of the ancient British barrow. The famous Smith-Mortimer succession case comes also within this period, and so does the tracking and arrest of Huret, the Boulevard assassin, an exploit which won for Holmes an autograph letter of thanks from the French President and the Order of the Legion of Honour.'

Dr Watson, 'The Golden Pince-Nez'

December 21st

At the single table sat the man whom we had seen in the street, with his evening paper spread out in front of him, and as he looked up at us it seemed to me that I had never looked upon a face which bore such marks of grief, and of something beyond grief – of a horror such as comes to few men in a lifetime.

'The Stockbroker's Clerk'

December 22nd

'I saw no more of Holmes during the day, but I could well imagine how he spent it, for Langdale Pike was his human book of reference upon all matters of social scandal. This strange, languid creature spent his waking hours in the bow window of a St James's Street club, and was the receiving-station, as well as the transmitter, for all the gossip of the Metropolis. He made, it was said, a four-figure income by the paragraphs which he contributed every week to the garbage papers which cater for an inquisitive public. If ever, far down in the turbid depths of London life, there was some strange swirl or eddy, it was marked with automatic exactness by this human dial upon the surface. Holmes discreetly helped Langdale to knowledge, and on occasion was helped in turn.'

Dr Watson, 'The Three Gables'

_____

_____

_____

_____

_____

_____

December 23rd

'Which of you gentlemen is Masser Holmes?' he asked.

Holmes raised his pipe with a languid smile.

'Oh! it's you, is it?' said our visitor, coming with an unpleasant, stealthy step round the angle of the table. 'See here, Masser Holmes, you keep your hands out of other folks' business. Leave folks to manage their own affairs. Got that, Masser Holmes?'

'The Three Gables'

December 24th

'It was on a Sunday evening that I received one of Holmes's laconic messages: "Come at once if convenient – if inconvenient come all the same. S. H." The relations between us in those latter days were peculiar. He was a man of habits, narrow and concentrated habits, and I had become one of them. As an institution I was like the violin, the shag tobacco, the old black pipe, the index books, and others perhaps less excusable. When it was a case of active work and a comrade was needed upon whose nerve he could place some reliance, my role was obvious.'

Dr Watson, 'The Creeping Man'

December 25th

He was a tall, handsome youth about thirty, well dressed and elegant, but with something in his bearing which suggested the shyness of the student rather than the self-possession of the man of the world. He shook hands with Holmes, and then looked with some surprise at me . . .

'Have no fear, Mr Bennett. Dr Watson is the very soul of discretion, and I can assure you that this is a matter in which I am very likely to need an assistant.'

'The Creeping Man'

December 26th

'But apart from this I had uses. I was a whetstone for his mind. I stimulated him. He liked to think aloud in my presence. His remarks could hardly be said to be made to me – many of them would have been as appropriately addressed to his bedstead – but none the less, having formed the habit, it had become in some way helpful that I should register and interject. If I irritated him by a certain methodical slowness in my mentality, that irritation served only to make his own flame-like intuitions and impressions flash up the more vividly and swiftly. Such was my humble role in our alliance.'

Dr Watson, 'The Creeping Man'

_____

_____

_____

_____

_____

_____

_____

_____

December 27th

Once only we saw a trace that someone had passed that perilous way before us. From amid a tuft of cotton grass which bore it up out of the slime some dark thing was projecting. Holmes sank to his waist as he stepped from the path to seize it, and had we not been there to drag him out he could never have set his foot upon firm land again. He held an old black boot in the air.

The Hound of the Baskervilles

December 28th

'There is no branch of detective science which is so important and so much neglected as the art of tracing footsteps. Happily, I have always laid great stress upon it, and much practice has made it second nature to me. I saw the heavy footmarks of the constables, but I saw also the track of the two men who had first passed through the garden. It was easy to tell that they had been before the others, because in places their marks had been entirely obliterated by the others coming upon the top of them. In this way my second link was formed, which told me that the nocturnal visitors were two in number, one remarkable for his height (as I calculated from the length of his stride) and the other fashionably dressed, to judge from the small and elegant impression left by his boots.'

Sherlock Holmes, *A Study in Scarlet*

December 29th

A flower-bed extended up to the study window, and we all broke into an exclamation as we approached it. The flowers were trampled down, and the soft soil was imprinted all over with footmarks. Large, masculine feet they were, with peculiarly long, sharp toes. Holmes hunted about among the grass and leaves like a retriever after a wounded bird. Then, with a cry of satisfaction, he bent forward and picked up a little brazen cylinder.

'I thought so,' said he; 'the revolver had an ejector, and here is the third cartridge. I really think, Inspector Martin, that our case is almost complete.'

'The Dancing Men'

December 30th

'To the man who loves art for its own sake,' remarked Sherlock Holmes, tossing aside the advertisement sheet of the *Daily Telegraph*, 'it is frequently in its least important and lowliest manifestations that the keenest pleasure is to be derived. It is pleasant to me to observe, Watson, that you have so far grasped this truth that in these little records of our cases which you have been good enough to draw up, and, I am bound to say, occasionally to embellish, you have given prominence not so much to the many *causes célèbres* and sensational trials in which I have figured, but rather to those incidents which may have been trivial in themselves, but which have given room for those faculties of deduction and of logical synthesis which I have made my special province.'

December 31st

'And yet,' said I, smiling, 'I cannot quite hold myself absolved from the charge of sensationalism . . .'

'You have erred, perhaps . . .

'It seems to me that I have done you full justice in the matter,' I remarked with some coldness, for I was repelled by the egotism which I had more than once observed to be a strong factor in my friend's character.

'No, it is not selfishness or conceit,' said he, answering, as was his wont, my thoughts rather than my words. 'If I claim full justice for my art, it is because it is an impersonal thing – a thing beyond myself. Crime is common. Logic is rare. Therefore it is upon the logic rather than upon the crime that you should dwell. You have degraded what should have been a course of lectures into a series of tales.'

Holmes and Watson, 'The Copper Beeches'